A GHOST IN THE ATTIC

SOLOMON PETCHERS

**If you enjoyed this book
thank Mrs. Wilcox for the donation!**

A Ghost in the Attic

ISBN 9781090778727

FOREWORD

The year is 2019. I wrote *A Ghost in the Attic* twenty years ago never really thinking I would ever get it published. It was a story reserved for my students and my own children. I've always enjoyed the craft of storytelling. Whenever I return to the attic after not visiting for long periods of time, I realize that this story is so much more than originally anticipated. The attic allowed me to make sense of some feelings about my childhood. Most of those feelings were good, but there were some that I wrestled with. The death of my father. My mother's reaction to his death. My own personal physical illness. On the outside, I learned to hide behind a sense of humor and surface encounters. On the inside, there was a struggle to make sense of things and the timing of those events. The attic, simple in its style and storytelling, is a special place where I learned to overcome the obstacles life put in my way and to use the lessons I've learned for some good in this crazy world. It's my wish that the journey into the attic offers something for you.

CHAPTER ONE

NEW BEGINNINGS

WHEN I REFLECT on everything that happened, I guess I can say that I knew from the very first night that something was different about my house. I don't mean in appearance; it looked just like every other house I've ever seen or been in. Down the block, the community resembled other communities back in Ohio. When looking down the street, it was like most streets where most of the houses appeared the same. And, just like every neighborhood, there was that one house that was more unkempt than the other houses. The lawn was overgrown, as if it hadn't been mowed in ages, and the bushes and ivy that crept up the side of the house had somehow molded into one indescribable mound of foliage that looked as if it could come alive at any moment. Now, I'm getting ahead of myself. Yes, my house was certainly different. No, it wasn't overgrown ivy or an uncut lawn that made my house different from the cookie-cutter houses that lined the street. Rather, it's what was living, or not really *living* at all, in the attic that separated my house from any other house I've ever been in. Of course, every ghost story has a beginning and here is mine.

———————

"Samson! Samson! Let's go. You're going to be late," my mother's voice called from the bottom of the stairs. As I tossed and turned, my aching muscles reminded me of the past few days I'd spent lifting and unpacking boxes. I quickly put that to the back of my mind as the rich aroma of bacon began to fill my room. I hopped out of bed and got ready for my first day at my new school. I couldn't imagine anything more horrible than being the new kid. I was against the move from the beginning, but Mom's boyfriend, Scott, had been asked to be the lead on his company's expansion into the San Diego area. Mom and I drove out to our new home and met the moving truck four days later. Scott had to stay and tie up a few loose ends. Mom joked that it was "so convenient" that he stayed behind because he wouldn't have to be part of unpacking all those boxes. So, here we were; uprooted from everything I'd known back in Ohio. I voiced my resistance but gave in to the fact that I was outnumbered, and this was how it was going to be. Anyway, I'd be lying if a part of me wasn't a little curious about starting over in a new place after a few years of bad memories.

When I was ready, I bounded down the stairs, pausing only long enough to look over the living room where there were still lots of boxes left to be unpacked. I knew what I was going to be doing over the next few days after school. Well, at least I would have something to do since I didn't have any friends yet. I made my way into the kitchen to find Mom rummaging through her camera bag and portfolio. She had made a decent living as a photographer back in Ohio—where she shot everything from weddings to family portraits. She had an interesting way of even turning the ugliest of kids into cute ones.

"Morning, Mom," I said as I tore open the wrapping around the package of paper plates and grabbed one.

"Hey there!" She spoke without looking up. "How'd ya sleep? I tell you what, this fresh west coast air helped me sleep like a newborn baby."

"Don't babies wake up all night?" I snickered. Mom didn't laugh. She was too busy organizing her work for the day. Finally, she clicked the snaps on her portfolio and turned her attention to me.

"So, did you answer my question?"

I stopped in the middle of pulling a few strips of bacon and some eggs out of the pan, "What was your question again?"

"How'd ya sleep?" Mom repeated as she took a seat at the table pushing the smaller moving boxes to one side.

"I guess I slept alright," I said as I slid into the seat at the breakfast nook. "I woke up a few times because I thought I kept hearing howling or something."

"It was probably just the wind blowing through the cracks in the house. This house is a little older than most." She pushed a tuft of hair from my face. "Don't be scared. It isn't that different than our house in Ohio. You'll just have to get used to the noises."

"I'm not scared," I answered in a mildly defensive tone. And the truth was that I wasn't, not in the least. The funny thing was, I didn't remember it being windy last night. Then again, it was a long, long day. Unless I was so delirious and tired from moving and unpacking that I was imagining it. But, even if I missed it, obviously my mother recalled it being windy. "So, you heard it too?"

"Heard what?"

"The howling."

She thought for a moment, "Well, yeah, I heard something. Like I said, it was probably the wind. You are just going through the new house jitters. Just relax, I'm right down the hall. I'm not going anywhere." She pinched my cheeks like I was a toddler.

"Mom. Stop. I'm not scared of anything," I laughed, still offended at the notion.

She smiled at me and changed the subject, "You ready for school?"

"Yup. How different could things be in the 5th grade here than they were at my old school?" I put my hands in the air and rolled my eyes.

"Probably not much different," Mom responded, not catching my sarcasm, which was a surprise because she was always calling me out about being too sarcastic.

I got up and put my plate in the trash. Things could be very different. At my old school, I knew pretty much everyone. That's not to say I was the popular kid, but I was friendly to everyone and people seemed to want to hang out with me. What if Southern California kids were different than kids in Ohio? My mother must have sensed something was on my mind.

"Hey, Sporto. Everything okay?"

I took one last sip of orange juice. "I don't know. It's this whole starting a new school thing. At home, school was a place where I belonged. It was all familiar to me. The people there were really good to us, especially after Dad died. They really helped us get through some tough times. And, now, well, it's like starting completely over and the whole idea just – just stinks if I think about it long enough."

The expression on her face changed like it did when she was thinking back to when things weren't so good. She tried to hide the tears filling her eyes. "Samson, new beginnings are exciting if you just give them a chance. I know we've been through a rough patch. But things have been looking up in the last year. Haven't they? We've had little successes along the way that have led us here. The only thing I ask is that you give it a chance."

"But what if I don't fit in here? What if I have no friends, especially like the ones back home?"

She cupped my face with both hands. "Let me ask you this. Back in Ohio, did you just find your friends along the side of the road somewhere?"

"No," I laughed having a feeling where she was going with this.

"Well, you didn't find them on eBay either. So, to make friends you are going to have to be your fun self and just go out and make some." She looked down at her watch as her eyes widened, "Oh my gosh, we are going to be late. You don't want to miss your bus and I don't want to miss my interview."

I watched her as she gathered her things. She tried to show me that things were going to work out for the best despite the struggles our family went through. While my dad was in the middle of his battle with cancer, she tried to be strong for him and me. It wasn't until after he passed that she finally allowed herself to be sad. That sadness turned into something else. It was a rough time for us, and it took some time for her to recover. So, when she started dating Scott a little over a year ago, I was okay with it because he's good to her. As long as she's happy, I'm okay with him, even though we had to uproot from Ohio and move here. "Mom?"

"Yeah, Sport?"

"Thanks," I smiled at her and she flashed a contented smile right back.

"Thank me later. We gotta hustle!"

CHAPTER TWO

STRANGE THINGS

I STOOD outside our front door and gave my mom a wave as she drove off. I surveyed the neighborhood for a moment. Remember that one house I mentioned that didn't look like it was very well taken care of? Well, that house happened to be right next to us. It looked like a jungle! The bushes that separated our two front yards were completely overgrown; they were creeping into our yard and had weeds that were breaking through the cracks in the driveway as if frozen mid-explosion. The leafless overhanging branches hung over into our yard and reminded me of the types of scratches a lion makes in the jungle to mark its territory. The tall grass flowed with the wind like the ocean.

The only thing I could think was that I was glad that I didn't have to mow it. In the last year that became my responsibility at home. If someone told me to mow that yard, they'd have to send a search party for me!

I zipped up my hoodie against the chilly April morning and made the first steps toward my new life at my new school.

⌐ the bottom step of the porch and headed towards the ⌐s stop. The foggy air added to the mystery of the day as the sun pierced little fingers of light through it. I was the first to arrive at the bus stop, of course. It wasn't long before the other kids started to arrive.

The first images that came through the mist were two girls, younger than me, walking side by side in perfect unison – left, right, left, right. They stopped about ten feet away from me and just stared— an uncomfortable stare that seemed to last forever. They were twins. The kind that insisted on matching everything from their red, knee-length coats to matching shoulder length hairstyles with a little curl at the ends. Then, just as quickly as they had stopped, they continued walking, brushing right past me. I gazed after them and watched as they parked on the sidewalk and leaned up against the chain link fence that bordered the house on the corner. I turned my back on them, but I could still feel them peering at me, pointing their judging fingers. I took a quick peek over my shoulder and yup, I was right.

I looked down for a moment, noticing the new scuffs on my shoes. When I looked up, I saw a large figure cutting a path through the morning fog. It appeared to temporarily grow thicker around the figure. It was a boy, a big boy, probably the biggest kid I had ever seen. He lumbered with a walk that really had no purpose. The combination of his slow, awkward walk and way the fog parted around him reminded me of the zombie movies Scott had gotten me hooked on. I chuckled to myself while keeping an eye on this big kid in the red and black flannel with a baseball cap pulled down over his eyes. Long, coarse, shoulder-length hair fanned out on all sides of his face.

Suddenly, the big kid's pace began to quicken as he

focused in on me. It looked like he had no intention of stopping. I could sense the girls, who had been busy pointing their fingers at me, stop and wait for the collision. The menacing figure closed in quickly. I closed my eyes waiting for the blow. Nothing. By now, I had expected my butt to be firmly planted on the ground, but instead, when I opened my eyes, I was staring into a black t-shirt which peeked through the open buttons of his flannel. Now, I'm not a big fan of daily showers, but even I could tell it was time for this kid to take one. I could feel his warm breath blowing down on me out of his nostrils.

I looked up at him, trying to find his eyes, but only found a dark shadow. I tried to smile at him and quickly come up with something clever to say but nothing came out. Suddenly, his lips parted, "You the kid who moved into the old Henderson house?" His voice came out hoarsely.

"Umm...what?" The only words I could manage as sweat started to form on my forehead in little beads.

He gave an annoyed sigh and then repeated, "Are you the kid who moved into the old Henderson house?"

"Well," this time I managed more, "I'm not really sure what you are talking about." I felt my body quiver in fear but didn't want to show it.

The big kid adjusted his footing to a more agitated stance which made me even more nervous. I looked back at the two girls and found them with their mouths wide open in utter shock. "Did you move into the green house near the end of the block or not?" he growled.

"Yeah, I guess so."

"Tsk," his lips smacked like he was eating peanut butter. "That's the old Henderson house," he grumbled in annoyance. "You don't know much about that house, do you?"

At that very moment, my sarcastic side came out unexpectantly, "Well, I do know it's a house. What's more to know?" As soon as I said it, I regretted it. Why did I have a habit of doing things like that? My mouth always seemed to get me in trouble. Now, I was using it with this kid who could easily pummel me with one hand tied behind his back.

"Well," he paused. "*Strange things* happen there. Three families in four years. Wouldn't you say that's strange?" I wasn't sure if he wanted an answer. Before I could speak, he grunted, "That's what's to know." He brushed past me, nearly cork-screwing me into the ground.

I stood there, speechless, half because I was dizzy and half because I was scared. What did he mean *strange things happen there*? I mean seriously!? And, what kind of kid introduces himself to a stranger like that? I felt my fear start to transform itself into bravery. I wanted answers and that's what I planned on getting. I spun around quickly to confront this kid. He was crouched down next to a tree with a thick stick in his hands. He looked at me from the dark regions of his cap and snapped that stick in his hands while curling the sides of his lips. I froze for a moment — picturing my smaller body as that stick. I needed information, but I figured it could wait, for now. I slowly turned back around, probably not hiding the fear on my face very well.

I didn't have much time to think about how I was going to find out about the '*strange things*' that happen in my house before a gray station wagon pulled up across the street. The rear passenger door opened, and a shoe stepped to the ground. As the other shoe made contact with the pavement, a head fashioned with large glasses peered out from behind the open door as he examined the bus stop. The boy stepped away from the car and pushed the door shut. He wore a blue ski jacket that was a bit much for April. He extended the arm of his rolling backpack, adjusted his glasses, and made his way to where we were all waiting. The others weren't falling over themselves to make him feel welcome. They didn't with me either, but I shouldn't have expected anything else. I was the new kid.

As the gray station wagon drove off, it gave a hearty beep of its horn at which the boy spun around quickly to wave enthusiastically and awkwardly. The boy in those thick eyeglasses started to walk towards me, surprised that there was someone new at the bus stop. Just as he was about to speak, a deep growl rose up behind him which caused the both of us to freeze up. I shifted my weight to look around the boy and there it stood. A black, short-haired dog growling, bearing his yellow tinted teeth. The hair on its back bristled and his head lowered as if he were going to attack.

I looked behind me and the two girls were nestled up against the fence. I quickly scanned to find the big kid and he was nowhere to be seen. Just then, I noticed his red flannel poorly camouflaged in the bushes on the other side of the fence that lined the house. How did he get over there so quickly? I thought. He moved pretty fast for a clumsy looking fellow. I wish I was there with him. But, for this little kid and me, there was no quick escape. The dog was too close and appeared too angry to make any sudden moves.

I grabbed the kid by his oversized ski coat and pulled him slowly, and cautiously, towards me. The dog did not like the movement whatsoever. His growl turned into a loud, ferocious bark. I had to act quickly, but not carelessly. With the boy close to me, I scooted him around my body with my right arm, so he ended up behind me.

Now there was nothing between the dog and me, and the

kid was safe. The dog stopped barking but continued a deep, menacing growl. Carefully, I stepped back to the edge of the curb, keeping the kid behind me, and squatted down to pick up the sticks that big kid had been snapping in his hands. The dog's eyes traced my every move — never letting up his growl. Slowly, regaining my stance, I never took my eyes off the dog, but careful not to lock eyes. Instead, I kept my stare just below his, showing that I wasn't a threat to him. With one of the sticks above my head, I prayed that he wouldn't think I was raising it against him. He must have though, because his growls once again turned into barks. My next move would be a critical one. If I just threw the stick, he may think I was going to whack him with it. Some type of distraction was needed. My lips pursed in an attempt to whistle the type of whistle a dog would think is friendly. Nothing really came out on the first try because my mouth was as dry as a desert. On the second try, a dull whistle barely made its way from my lips. At first it had no effect, but upon the third try, he shifted his head from right to left but was still growling. I whistled again which silenced the dog. This was my chance, I launched the stick. The dog, confused, watched it sail over his shoulder and land on the street. Turning his attention back to me, he growled again a little less ferociously. I whistled again while raising the second stick over my head calling to the dog, "Here boy. C'mon. You wanna play?" Nervously, I called to the beast, causing him to tilt his head back and forth again. When I threw it, he ran after it, sniffed and then picked it up in between his teeth, and trotted over to me. He, with the same caution I had about him, dropped the stick at my feet. After a couple of rounds, the hair on the dog's neck wasn't standing up any longer, his expression had softened, and he appeared like a puppy that didn't want our game to end. I reached into my backpack to retrieve my roast beef sandwich I had hastily made the night before. He watched me slightly more cautiously than he did a second ago. I asked, "Hey boy, you want some?" The dog moved closer as I tore off a piece. He sniffed and took the offering from me. With my palm up, I reached out to the dog. He gave my hand a lick. I moved my hand slowly to the top of his head and gave him a scratch, which he really enjoyed, as he moved closer to me. The two girls and the boy with the glasses looked on with amazement.

Just then, the bus pulled up. The other kids were nailed down with fear. Recognizing their caution, I coaxed the dog out of the way. He was like a completely different beast as he trotted at my heels and sat down next to me. The two girls filed their way toward the bus with their mouths hanging open. Next, the boy with the thick-lensed glasses walked on the bus with the same look. Finally, that big kid, who I couldn't recall jumping back over the fence, lumbered his way onto the bus, all while carefully watching the dog. Suddenly, the dog started to growl and ferociously bark again, and so the big kid hustled on as quickly as possible. Weird, I thought. I knelt down to eye level with the dog, now knowing that I was out of danger, "I'd bark at that kid too, if I could." I chuckled to myself as I started to board the bus. The dog stared at me sad and confused. "I'll be back." He jumped up on hind legs and showered my face with kisses. After getting him to stop, I patted him again on the head and entered the bus. As it started to drive away, the dog chased us but gave up shortly afterwards putting his head down as if he was missing someone.

CHAPTER THREE

THE BOY WITH THE THICK GLASSES

ON THE BUS, the pickings were slim. Sure, there were some seats available, but no one was going out of their way to let the new kid have a seat. There were two options from what I could see. The first was to sit next to that big kid and try to find out what the heck he was talking about at the bus stop; the second was to sit next the other boy from the bus stop and find out what his story was. With the opportunity presenting itself, I decided, nervously, to reach out to that big kid. As I approached him, he clamped his hat over his eyes with his enormous paws, practically on top of his nose, and curled up his lip like the dog did at the bus stop. His look halted my steps. This was one beast I'd have to try to tame another day.

Before I even resolved to go with option two, a nasally voice pierced the air, "Hey you, new kid. This seat is open."

I looked up and pointed to myself as if to say *are you talking to me?*

"Phyllis won't let you stand the whole way and it looks like you don't have much of a choice," his voice sounded as if air was slowly being released from an inflated balloon. The boy in the thick classes peered over a comic book.

As I walked past where the two girls from the bus stop were seated, I noticed they were still judging me. I surveyed my options one last time before I sat down with the boy and his thick glasses. This was not exactly how my first day had played out in my head.

The nasally voice greeted me, "Hi, I'm Nathaniel. Nathaniel Fargo. I'm in the 3rd grade. What's your name?"

"Umm...I'm Samson. Samson O'Keefe. 5th grade. Nice to meet you." I looked over my shoulder to keep track of that big kid, not really paying much attention to Nathaniel.

"Nice to meet ya. It was pretty amazing the way you handled Spike this morning."

"Huh? What do you mean?"

"Hello?" Nathaniel threw his hands up in disbelief. "Spike? The savage beast of a dog at the bus stop this morning?" He made his best angry dog-face and let out a *grrr*. "I think you saved my life."

"Oh him? He seemed like a nice dog once I got him to trust me. He was definitely spooked by something."

Nathaniel smacked himself on his forehead in astonishment, "Umm...I don't think you understand. That dog has been terrorizing our bus stop for years. I heard he made off with one of the kids a few years back, and they never found him again."

I rolled my eyes knowing that his story couldn't possibly be true. It was then that I noticed one of the two girls from the bus stop looking back at me. "What's up with those girls? They are totally weird," I asked Nathaniel, pointing at them.

"Oh, that would be Jan and Pam. They are never apart. Twins. They don't really talk to anybody, but they are always pointing their fingers and whispering like they are judging people. Don't let them bother you."

That explains a lot, I thought to myself as I shrugged my shoulders like it was no big deal. My mind shifted to the other kid at the bus stop, and I looked over my shoulder again for some reason expecting him to sneak up on me.

"So, where did you move from?"

"We moved from Ohio. A town outside of Akron." His piercing tone was really starting to get to me. Just then, my mother's conversation with me this morning came into focus. *So, to make friends you are going to have to be your fun-self and just go out and make some.* This was proving to be harder than I originally thought.

"So, which house is yours?" Nathaniel asked.

"The green and white one down towards the end of the block." The whole bus grew quiet for a moment as if everyone was eavesdropping into our conversation. I looked around half-expecting everyone to be peering at me. They weren't, but when I looked at Nathaniel, he was looking at me through those thick glasses that made his eyes look like alien eyes. His face, already pale, took on an inexplicable shade of white that I was sure no one had ever laid eyes on. His mouth, hanging open like a ventriloquist's dummy, exposed a mouthful of braces I hadn't noticed until now. "Hello?" I waved my hands in front of his eyes trying to break him out of this trance. "Hello? Nathaniel? Everything okay?"

He closed his mouth and swallowed hard. He blinked as if seeing me for the first time. His nasally voice came out raspy and slow as if each word was important, "Do you mean you moved into the old Henderson house?"

Now, he had my complete attention. "I guess so. I don't see what the big deal is. It's just a house."

He gulped, "It's *not* just a house."

"What do you mean it's *not* just a house?" My eyes pierced through Nathaniel's glasses into his hazel eyes.

"Well, of course it's a house," he patted his jeans, "but, it's not just *any* house."

"So, tell me what you know."

Nathaniel sat up straight as if struck by something. He assessed his knowledge quietly. He looked as if he were about to speak and then decided against it. Scratching his chin, he squeaked, "Actually, not too much. It has a bad history. I was just told that strange things happen there."

I felt my face redden a bit in frustration, but I contained myself, "I figured out that much at the bus stop from that big kid in the red and black flannel." I threw a thumb over my shoulder and whispered, "What's his story?"

Nathaniel adjusted his glasses and matched my whisper, "Oh, you would be referring to Moose. He's been here as long as I can remember. He's the biggest kid in the entire school. No one talks to him, and he doesn't talk to anyone." Then, he paused as if hearing me for the first time. "Do you mean he spoke to you? I didn't think he could talk. One time I think I heard him grunt but that's it."

I whispered a little louder, "Uh, yeah. After he nearly knocked me over."

"What did he say?"

I glanced behind me to make sure he wasn't standing over me. "Like I said, he said strange things happen at my house and something about three families in four years. I don't even know what that means, do you? Who are the Hendersons?"

"Well, I can't really say who they are. Everything that happened, happened before I even realized something was happening. Got me?" Nathaniel's voice rose to its familiar nasally-piercing tone. Then, he brought it down again, "The person you should be asking is-," he gulped. "is Moose. He was here before everybody."

"Moose?"

"Yes, but good luck with that. One time I saw someone try to make conversation with him, and he just stared at him from the cave under his cap. Later on, that kid was found stuffed into a locker. It's a good thing he wasn't hurt. But his parents pulled him out of the school lickity split." He snapped his finger as if performing a magic trick.

I sat mostly silent for the remainder of the ride to school while I thought of a way I could get information about the old Henderson house – my home. It was my right to know. Wasn't I the one who had to live there? I turned to look back at Moose for moment. How was I going to get the information I needed without getting stuffed into a locker? As the new kid at school, it may take hours, perhaps days, before anyone even knew I was missing. The thought sent shivers down my spine.

CHAPTER FOUR

MUSIC CLASS

THE MORNING FOG parted as we pulled into Shadow Rock Elementary. I peered out of the window at my new surroundings, wondering how different things could be here. Honestly, I wasn't in a rush to get off the bus. My first day hadn't started off too awesomely. While I said goodbye to Nathaniel, I fished out the schedule from my pocket to find out where my classroom was. As I approached the room, I took a few deep breaths before peeking in. Inside the class, there were kids packed in groups of threes and fours talking and laughing. My first step in hit some type of pause button – nearly every kid in the room focused on me which caused my throat to go completely dry. The teacher must have noticed the silence and lifted her head to see what was going on. "Ahh, you must be our new student." She shuffled papers on her desk, "Let's see. Where is my list?"

"O'Keefe," I choked out.

"Excuse me?" she looked confused.

"My name is O'Keefe. Samson O'Keefe."

"Ahh, yes, here it is. You're right. That's your name," she replied with a smile. "I'm Mrs. Westphal." She turned her attention to the rest of the class as the morning bell chimed the official start of the day, "All right class. Please find your seats. C'mon, quickly now. We have a lot to take care of today." The class finally filed into their seats, which were organized into rows, and gave Mrs. Westphal their attention – well at least most of them. "Please help me welcome Samson O'Keebler." A few of the kids chuckled.

"O'Keefe. Samson O'Keefe," I corrected her trying my best not to make a big deal that she just completely butchered my name.

"Oh, I'm so sorry. Samson O'Keefe."

It was then that I noticed out of the corner of my eye a familiar black and red flannel. Moose. He looked pretty disinterested in what was happening. I couldn't tell whether this was a good omen or a bad one.

The class's greeting was lukewarm at best. Mrs. Westphal changed her focus to her desk once again, "Ahh, this is nearly perfect. You can have a seat right in front of Norman. There's been a vacant seat there since January."

I nodded. Norman? Really? Sounds like another Nathaniel. This day definitely wasn't getting any better. The only thing was that there were a few empty seats, so I didn't know which one to take. So, I waited.

"Norman," Mrs. Westphal called out as she adjusted her glasses, "Norman, please raise your hand so we can get Samson settled in." The classroom grew awkward and coldly quiet. I looked around waiting. Mrs. Westphal spoke more firmly, "Norman Oleadertag. Please raise your hand so we can get Samson a seat. Let's not have a continuation of last week."

Finally, a hand lazily rose into the air. My eyes opened

wide and my stomach grew sick. The raised hand was attached to Moose's arm. Shakily, I walked towards my new desk, I searched for Moose's eyes, but they remained buried under his cap. When I sat down, something funny hit my thoughts. *Moose's real name was Norman? Norman Oleadertag?* That was like one of those oxymoron things where two opposite words make up a word like jumbo shrimp. Moose sounded so intimidating and Norman Oleadertag seemed so, well, geeky.

Have you ever said something that you wished you could take back as soon as it spilled out of your mouth? Well, what happened next was one of those moments. I was so deep in thought at Moose's real name that I turned around, looked squarely at him and asked, "Norman? How did you go from being Norman to being named Moose?" His lips tightened as he pulled the brim of his cap, with a skateboarding skeleton on it, closer over his nose. I wanted to take the words back, but it was too late. I wanted to say that I was just kidding, but the damage was done. Slowly, I turned around, my face red. As I did, it looked as if every kid in class had witnessed what just happened. Oh boy, oh boy.

I sat with the heavy weight of what I did for the first thirty minutes. It wasn't until Mrs. Westphal arranged the class into groups of four and five kids to work on a project that I felt my sense of dread lighten. Thank goodness, Moose and I weren't assigned the same group, but throughout the course of time, I glanced over to where his group was working. He just sat there while all the other kids cautiously worked around him. It must be hard for him to make any friends being like that. I'm sure there was not a kid in the entire school that would even think of approaching him.

When my focus shifted back to my group and the poster project on states and capitals, the kids showed genuine interest in getting to know me. That helped, but I couldn't understand why or how I put myself in such a bad spot with Moose. I'll probably never learn about the strange things that happened in my house now because my new, *new* home would be in the comforts of a locker.

Just then, the bell rang, and Mrs. Westphal reminded the class that today was chorus and the ensuing collective groan led me to believe that everyone had the same feelings I did about it. I thought to myself, *do they really want to hear me sing?*

I waited until everyone moved to the door and found my place at the end of one of the two lines. Mrs. Westphal asked me to switch the lights and off we went. Our walk down the hallway was surprisingly quiet. My old school was never like this. On the opposite side of the hallway, walking toward us, were Jan and Pam walking in perfect unison. They met my eyes for a moment and didn't even crack a smile.

Finally, we arrived at the band/chorus room. I waited until everyone filed in and found my place at the end of the middle row. Ms. Rodda, the choir teacher, remained in the hallway talking with Mrs. Westphal. She popped her head in the classroom because she could hear us getting loud. "Hello, cherubs. I need to talk with your teacher for a moment. Sara, please come to the front and run us through our scales. I'll be just a minute. Thank you," she finished with a sing-songy voice.

What happened next happened so fast that I didn't have time to even react. The class went through their scales. I didn't even know what scales were, so I just stood there quietly examining the classroom. I swear the air chilled as the scales came to an eerie halt. And as I glanced to my right, the kids parted, tripping and falling forwards and backwards, and

22

coming through the middle of it all was Moose, as if he were crashing through bowling pins. He came right up to me again and grabbed a fistful of my shirt. He snarled, and in a raspy, agitated voice he growled, "You've got guts, but definitely no brains." He pulled me closer like I was a ragdoll causing my limbs to flail. "I'll see you at lunch where we can—" he gave a pause, which I'm convinced was for dramatic effect, "be alone and discuss the matter further."

I swallowed hard and peered to my left and right to see all the other kids helplessly watching. Searching for his eyes, I looked up towards the darkness under his cap. He was definitely staring at me, I couldn't see it, but I could feel it. I felt as if I should at least say something, so I managed in the most sheepish, meek sounding voice, "I – I look forward to it?" He jerked me closer even though I thought it was physically impossible to do so. Then, just as suddenly, he shoved me back with one huge paw that sent me slamming into the kid behind me and knocking him off the risers.

Ms. Rodda walked into the room and asked us why we had stopped our warm ups. My stomach was in knots. *I'm a dead man* is all I kept thinking. *I'm a dead man.* Like I said, my mouth has a way of getting me in trouble, but this time it had *really* gotten me in some hot water.

For the rest of the class, time played tricks with my mind. One moment time continued at its normal speed and other times it seemed as if the morning was speeding by. I was completely distracted during chorus. I kept one watchful eye on where Moose was at all times. As the class ran through a song, his lips didn't part once except to yawn as boredom settled into him

CHAPTER FIVE

FREDDY SULLIVAN

LATER THAT DAY, I was right in the middle of a math problem when Mrs. Westphal's voice broke my concentration. "Alright everyone, can I have your eyes up here? It's that time again. Lunch time!" It was the first time the entire morning I actually hadn't been thinking about the impending doom that awaited me at lunch. Now was that time, I'd have to face whatever Moose wanted to discuss further. I followed the class down to the cafeteria, peering at the never-ending rows of cold, gray, steel lockers that lined the hallway. I wondered which one Moose would stuff me into. My mother joked that I always had a "flair for the dramatic." I chuckled to myself because this was one of those times. In all seriousness, this was about the worst first day of school for any kid, anywhere, period.

The cafeteria was a busy place. As I looked around trying to figure where to sit, I also searched for Moose. He was nowhere to be found. A few of the guys from class waved me over. "Hey, O'Keebler. Come over here."

"It's O'Keefe." I corrected without really correcting

anyone at all. I guess I'd have to live with that for a while. I walked over to the group. *There's safety in numbers, right?* I thought to myself.

I sat down next to a few kids who were bartering over lunches and poking jabs at each other. This was the only time of the day that actually felt like my old school. However, right in the middle of my first bite of what was left of the sandwich I shared with Spike earlier, the table grew awkwardly silent. I looked around at their faces. Judging me? It didn't appear that way. Finally, Billy, a skater-type kid with shoulder length hair, spoke what was on everyone's mind. "O'Keebler, what's going on between you and Moose?"

I reminded them of my name, but at that moment, they still weren't interested in getting it right.

"Yeah, I've never, and I mean NEVER, seen him that angry before. We've all heard the stories, but never actually saw it," a kid named Nick said. I panned their faces and they nodded in agreement. I swallowed the bite from my sandwich without chewing it.

"Well, as you saw. He's pretty upset with me. What's his problem?" I asked trying poorly to hide my concern for my own wellbeing.

"As you figured out already, he's the biggest kid in school," Billy said. "He came to our school a couple of years ago. The fourth grade?" He looked around at the other kids for confirmation. "Anyway, as soon as he came here, trouble started in for him. I mean, he caused most of it anyway. So, back to my question, what happened between you and Moose?"

I thought about what to say before blurting anything out that I didn't want to. "Well, I just... You see, he came up to me at the bus stop. Actually, he nearly knocked me over. He asked me a question and I-"

Billy grabbed my shoulder. "You mean to tell us that Moose Oleadertag spoke to you first? Holy cow!"

"Yeah, he doesn't speak to anyone really," another kid added. "You've seen him in class. He just kinda sits there and does nothing!"

"Well, he doesn't exactly do nothing," a kid named Christian added. "Remember Freddy Sullivan?" They all shook their heads as if they all remembered at the same time.

"What happened to Freddy Sullivan?" I asked, staring at them with real concern.

Nick took point in telling the story. "One day, last year, Freddy was walking down the hallway and Moose walked right up to him. Shoved him into the locker with a BLAM—"

"—and then shoved him *into* the locker," Christian said moving his arms as if he were pushing someone.

"And, trust me, Freddy wasn't a skinny kid. I heard it took some bacon grease to help him slip out," Billy interrupted.

"Bacon grease? Really?" Nick rolled his eyes and took over telling the story again, "After he slammed the door, he muttered, 'Next time, you'll do what I tell you to do.'"

I couldn't believe what I was hearing, not only because I may have been a little afraid this would happen to me, but it just didn't seem real. This Moose kid sounded crazier than he already appeared. "Well, what happened to Freddy Sullivan?" I asked.

These guys started looking around at each other like they weren't going to be the one that was going to tell me. I thought *Oh my gosh, Moose killed him.* So, finally I said, "C'mon guys. It couldn't be that bad." By the looks on their faces it was obvious that it was. It really was *that* bad.

Finally, Nick cleared his throat and spoke, "That's the weird part. You see, Principal Miller freed Freddy from his steel cell –"

"With bacon grease," Billy interrupted.

Nick rolled his eyes again and continued, "Dude, you're killing me with the bacon grease. Anyway, after Principal Miller freed Freddy, she asked him who had done that to him. For good reason, Freddy didn't want to tell. It may only make matters worse, right?" He looked around and the others nodded their heads in agreement.

"Somehow," Nick continued, "Miller convinced Freddy it would be okay if he told her who did it. Of course, Freddy said it was Moose. Freddy told us that Miller said Moose would not get away with that type of behavior and there would be major consequences for his actions. She also promised that he would be safe."

Tell you the truth, I'm not sure I would have told anyone if that happened to me if I was that kid. Moose didn't behave like your typical bully. "So, what happened next?"

Nick spoke, "The next day, Miller calls Moose into her office and slaps him with three days of in-school suspension."

I took a bite of my sandwich trying to digest the story these guys were telling me. Half of me wondered if it were even true, or perhaps, some kind of fairytale, myth, or urban legend. Billy took lead, "Everyone thought Freddy was crazy for telling on Moose. But Freddy kept on saying that Moose was getting exactly what he deserved and that he can't just walk around and get whatever he wants by force.

"So, for three days Freddy was safe. Even on the day Moose returned, it looked like everything was going to be okay," he paused, "That was until the dismissal bell rang."

"The hallways were what they always were at the end of

the day – a traffic jam," Nick continued. "Freddy was in the middle of the hall in a circle of friends when suddenly his books were knocked out of his hands. He bent over to pick up his stuff in that chaotic mess of kids moving back and forth through the hallways. What he didn't see, but every single kid in the hallway witnessed, was Moose, who's easily a whole foot taller than the tallest kid. He parts the entire hallway simply by walking. Kids moved to the left and right of the hall like he had some kind of special powers.

"All that craziness at the end of the day completely comes to a standstill. The only one talking is Freddy who is frantically trying to collect his books. 'Really? No one is going to help me?' He stood up annoyed and ready to badger his friends for not helping and instead found himself staring right into the chest of Moose," Nick said, putting his hand straight up to his nose as if it were Moose's chest. Then, he took a sip of his milk before continuing. "Some of the kids who had witnessed this close up, swear they saw that dark space up under Moose's cap shine green!"

Billy continued, "Yeah, but that part can't be true." He slapped Nick's arm.

"Oh, but bacon grease could be? You clearly have an unhealthy obsession with bacon grease!"

"How else would they get Freddy out?" Billy threw up his arms.

"Say what you want, but lots of people saw it."

"Oh please! Cary Jensen? That kid lies and cheats all the time. Haven't you seen him on the playground?"

"C'mon man, really? You're just saying that because he doesn't like—"

"Guys!" I interjected. "Can you debate this later? What the heck happened next?"

"Anyway," Billy continued looking at me, his eyes wide, "Freddy's body starts to shake. Moose bends over and whispers something into his ear. No one knows what he said, but Freddy instantly peed himself. Seriously, like a full puddle."

"Moose pushed past him and walked away."

"Well, what happened?" I asked in a combination of astonishment and disbelief.

"That's just it," Nick finished. "That was the last day we ever saw Freddy Sullivan."

"What the heck does that mean? The *last* day you saw him was that day?"

"Yeah, man. It was like he completely disappeared," Billy finished his sandwich while all the other kids sat back, exhausted from the story.

I sat there for a moment. Thinking. Wondering. A lot didn't add up. "So, what did Moose do, kill him? I mean what about his family? There are too many loose ends. This story cannot possibly be true."

"Dude, I was there," Billy insisted.

"Okay, maybe that part in the hallway actually happened, but the rest can't be true."

"Hey, believe what you want, but you need to be careful with this guy. You don't want to end up another Freddy Sullivan."

Nick put his hand on my shoulder and asked, "So, you said that Moose said something to you. What was it?"

Now all eyes were fixed on me. I waited a few seconds, deliberately, kind of enjoying the control. "He asked me something about the old Henderson home."

Each kid stopped what they were doing. The silence was awkward for a second and then, all at once, everyone asked me what I knew about the house. Billy stopped them,

"Samson. What do you know about the old Henderson house?"

I swallowed hard, "I don't know anything about it except..."

"Except what?" They all asked at once.

"Except that apparently—I live there."

"Shut your mouth right now!" Nick blurted in quiet excitement and disbelief. "Are you sure?"

"Well, that's just it. I'm not sure. I'm not sure about anything right now. All I know is that Moose came up to me at the bus stop and asked me about it. I wish I knew what the fuss was about."

"You mean you don't know?"

"The only other thing Moose said was something about three families in four years. So, NO, I don't know."

My audience grew quiet for a moment. Billy finally said, "Strange things happen there."

I felt my cheeks redden with frustration as if they were on fire. I slammed my hands on the table and with an agitated tone I exclaimed, "Yeah, this is the third time I've heard that *strange things* happen there. But, no one is willing to give a single piece of useful information about these so-called *strange things*! This school shouldn't be called Shadow Rock. It should be called Let's Be Vague To The New Kid About His New Creepy Little House Elementary School."

The table along with the rest of the entire cafeteria silenced. The boys just sat there, mouths agape. I stared back at them making sure I met all of their eyes. I didn't care. I was fired up. Just then, Billy cuts the tension and says, "Dude, don'tcha think that name is a little long for an elementary school?"

We all busted out laughing. I said my apologies while still

cracking up at my outburst. Finally, I said, "Seriously guys, I need to find out more information about my house. It's only fair. I'm the one that's gotta live there, right?"

As we stood up to head outside to recess, Billy and Nick put their hands on my shoulders. Nick spoke, "Listen man, I'm with ya. I'd want to know too, but from what I hear, the person you want to talk to is, well—"

"Moose, I know," I rolled my eyes.

"And, from what I heard in chorus class today, he wants to talk to you, too. I hope you didn't forget. No one would blame you for faking an illness or something."

It's true. I didn't forget about Moose wanting *to discuss the matter further*. It was time for recess and I hadn't seen him yet. He probably was going to talk with me outside.

"Oh, by the way," Billy added as we walked through the door that lead to the playground area. "Remember the story about Freddy Sullivan? Well, he used to live in the old Henderson house, too." He slapped me on the back and took off to meet the others.

I stopped dead in my tracks, dumbfounded, while the others ran outside to find their places at the wallball courts or to pick teams for kickball. I used to love recess. I used to love playing kickball. Today? I couldn't play. Not now. My brain raced to the point that it was starting to hurt. Questions whirled through my mind: What were these strange things that were going on in my house? Was it some strange coincidence that Freddy Sullivan lived in the same house that I live in now? Had Moose wanted to discuss the matter further with Freddy the same way he wants with me? Was there a cold locker with my name written all over it, or perhaps worse? Why had Moose singled me out? Everyone was afraid of Moose, but why was I the only one he's communicated with?

I looked around for Moose. We had an appointment, and he didn't strike me as the type to reschedule. I walked along the side of the building and looked out toward the field where a bunch of kids were engaged in a game of kickball. I still couldn't take my mind off the day. It weighed heavily on me. So much had happened since this morning, and I couldn't piece it together to make any sense whatsoever. What happened next just added to the inexplicable events of the day.

As I started to walk out towards the kickball game, something shoved me from behind knocking any air in my lungs out and me onto the ground in a heap. It had to be Moose, but I looked up, hoping it wasn't. With the sun behind him, Moose's massive frame cast an ominous shadow and swallowed any hint of light around me. It wasn't long before nearly the entire playground had found its way over to where Moose and I were. I watched as Billy and Nick and the others looked on helplessly, not joining into the quiet chant of *"Fight! Fight!"*

I made my way to my feet. I shuffled to my left and put my hands up the way Scott had taught me if I would ever need to defend myself. If Moose wanted a fight, I wasn't going to go down without the appearance of one. He didn't even put his hands into a fighting position. He just stared through those dark shadows. Once I put my hands up, he even smirked exposing a chipped tooth and chapped lips. He was going to enjoy this.

I wish I could say that I gave him a good fight. I continued to shuffle to the left as the "fight" chants grew louder. I clenched my fists and prepared to counter anything he would throw at me. That didn't work. With both hands, he shoved me again, hard, causing my back to slam against the wall knocking the air out of me for the second time. Then, he grabbed a fist full of my shirt again and dragged me to the end of the building and took me behind the corner. I tried to find my footing and pull away, but it was no good. I was going around the building with him whether I wanted to or not. But, before he did, he directed his attention toward the crowd of kids that had gathered around. "Stay!" he growled and put his huge, free hand up directing the kids to not even think about coming to watch.

Here's the inexplicable part I was telling you about. You see, he dragged me several more feet. I tried to fight him off, but it was no use. He was too big and angry to be reckoned with. He then stood me upright and just stared at me for a moment. The snarl on his lips disappeared and sort of a smile broke out on his face. At least, I thought it was an attempt at a smile. Boy, he was *really* going to enjoy this. Then, he let go of my shirt and put both massive hands on my shoulders. I cocked my head to the side, like a confused dog, trying to make sense of all this. His face, that looked so hard and calloused, looked like, well, a kid. A really big kid.

With his hands firmly clapped onto my shoulders he spoke, "You know, you are the first kid who ever spoke to me without looking afraid. I gotta say that after homeroom, I looked around for a nice cozy locker for you. But, the more I thought about it, I thought if this kid has the guts to stand up to me and say what was on his mind, then he just might be okay. You made an effort to talk to me, and believe me, that doesn't happen too often. So, I figured I'd give you a chance."

He loosened his grip on my shoulders which was a good thing because they were starting to go numb. I can't say I fully understood what the heck was going on. I straightened my shirt which was beyond looking neat at this point, and managed some words through my dry throat, "So, what does this mean?"

"It means I don't kick your butt. Isn't that enough?" Moose snarled out of a half-smile.

I shook my head earnestly, "Works for me."

Moose chuckled and pulled his cap closer over his eyes, "Relax. So, tell me something. What's it like living in the old Henderson place?"

I nodded my head not really knowing how to answer the question. "I don't understand what you mean. I don't understand what anyone means when they talk about my house. I guess it feels like any other home. I've only lived there a couple of days. Not much has happened."

"Not now anyway," Moose broke his concentration for a moment to look away as if he was thinking or picturing something. "That place ain't right."

"How do you mean?" I asked.

Moose grew more serious, "Are you sure you wanna know?" The truth was I was nervous about knowing, but I knew that I had to.

Those who waited around the corner of the building were completely shocked when Moose and I came around the corner side by side. I'm sure some expected to see Moose walk out by himself, and my body left in a heap. Together, we walked through the group of kids as they parted ways. I caught a glimpse of Billy. His face said it all. I looked at him and the others as I passed, threw my shoulders and hands up as if to say, *I have no idea what is going on either.*

Moose stopped halfway through the group of kids and tightened his lips as he looked over those who came to watch my extinction like they were finally getting an answer to how the dinosaurs disappeared. He adjusted his cap and looked as if he'd take on the entire group of kids if he had to. "Is there a problem?" Every eye looked away. "That's what I thought." He paused for a moment, purposely planning his next words. "Now MOVE!" His voice thundered, sending the crowd scrambling in every direction like when a drop of water falls on ants busy at work. Out of pure reaction, and let's be honest, there was fear involved, I started to move away too. Moose's hands found my shoulder again. "Not you, Samson," he said with a half-smile.

As I walked side by side with this kid who made everyone around him, me included, feel nervous and afraid, an unsettling feeling set into the pit of my stomach. I wasn't happy about it, but if this leads me to finding out about the old Henderson house, then I'd just have to deal with it.

CHAPTER SIX

THE BUS RIDE HOME

Moose and I hadn't said another word to each other the rest of the school day. The kids I ate lunch with; Billy, Nick, and the others didn't say too much to me either. I couldn't quite put my finger on it, but they kept their distance from me. It looked as if by receiving a pardon from my death sentence, the others issued a sentence of their own. I sure hoped they didn't perceive me as the same kind of person as Moose; a bully.

I had encountered a bully before. Stan Hanson. Moose dwarfed him by a good five inches, and like Moose, people avoided Stan. Like Moose, Stan instilled fear through a simple look. Like Moose, he could pummel just about anyone he wanted to. And, like Moose, Stan had no friends. At least Stan had the lackeys that hung around him like little minions. Moose? Moose flew solo.

I remember my mother telling me that Stan could have been the way he was because maybe he had some problems at home. Being a bully was his way to channel his anger and sadness. She said that some families have so many problems that kids get neglected or even abused. Every family was different.

I know that my home life wasn't always peachy. While my father was sick, my mother poured so much into trying to keep things normal. She tried to do everything she could to make sure I didn't miss school or flag football practice. For Dad, she cared for him nearly twenty-four hours a day, every single day. After he died, everything changed for a while. My mother went into a pretty deep depression. There were days were I barely ever saw her. She'd remain holed away in her room. I spent a lot of time with friends and family, passed around like some kind of dinner plate. I was angry with her for a while. Hadn't she known that I lost someone too? I was mad because I still needed someone to explain things to me. I was only 7 years old. Too young to try to make sense of what was happening on my own. We had spent the greater part of six months visiting hospitals, sleeping at hospitals, and eating hospital food. It was like I lost both parents. Obviously, my mother found herself again, and we went to counseling to come to terms with my dad's death, but also to repair our relationship.

My point of telling this is that I do remember being mad all the time and wanting to be alone during that ordeal. So, if Moose and Stan were kids who did have problems at home, I could certainly understand what they were feeling. But, I had never had the urge outright pick on or beat up someone. I never channeled my anger in that way. I guess each person is different.

So, what problems did Moose have at home to cause him to be the way he is? Finding the answer to that certainly could explain things. I had seen something today that was different than what 99% of the school probably saw. Moose did have a softer side to him. I wasn't sure if I'd see it again, but he said we were cool, and for now that was good enough for me.

Like I said, the day was pretty quiet after that. Well, except for when the bell signaling the end of the day went off. Moose's body jolted awake after a cat nap and he yelled, "Okay Mom!" The class didn't quite know how to react to it. If they laughed too loudly, Moose might find a locker for them. Instead, most of the class just snickered and exited the classroom.

I wasn't sure if I should wait for Moose, but when I looked back through the sea of kids, there he was laboring through the halls the same way when I first met him at the bus stop that morning. No rush. Moving at his own pace. I swam back through the crowd like a salmon swimming upstream and finally reached him.

"Did you have a nice nap?" I asked him nervously.

Moose's head looked in my direction. He clapped his cap tighter on his head as a slight smile broke across his face. "Was I snoring?" He ran his fingers through the length of his hair, embarrassed.

I chuckled, "Not too loudly. You only blew out one of my ear drums." We both laughed. By the looks of things, the entire school fixed their eyes on us. Even Principal Miller looked surprised. I'm guessing not many people had even seen Moose smile in a long time.

Just then a nasally voice cut through the air, "Hey Samson, what's so funny? Nathaniel looked up at me and was surprised to see Moose walking by my side.

"Oh, hey Nathaniel. How's it going?" I looked up to see if Moose had noticed him. There was no telling if he did, but the smile was gone from his face. He was back in Moose-mode.

"Moose and I were just laughing at something that happened in-"

Just then, Moose nudged my arm and whispered, "Samson...don't." Then he sped up his walk and moved ahead of us.

I looked down at Nathaniel, "Listen Nathaniel, I'll talk to you later." I directed my attention to where Moose was and raced to catch up. "Moose wait up. C'mon."

Nathaniel called after me, panicked, "Was it something I said?"

I finally caught up with Moose, "Hey. C'mon. Wait up. What happened back there? You alright?"

"Yeah, how do you mean?"

"Well, it was like something back there bothered you. What's up?"

Remaining serious, he said, "Forget about that. You can't understand, okay? Just forget about it."

"What's that supposed to mean? I'm not an idiot, ya know."

Moose grew more upset. "Listen, Samson. I told you that you and I are cool. Now just forget about it."

It was clear that something was wrong. But he didn't seem angry. I couldn't figure it out. I thought it best to just let it go. "Well, I'll forget about it...for now."

"That's what I figured," Moose said as he got on the bus.

The bus ride was chaotic. Moose and I sat together quietly across the aisle while a bunch of the other kids were jumping around like animals. Phyllis wasn't happy, as she threatened a half a dozen times that she was "this close" to turning the bus around and heading back to school. Apparently, this was a threat that no one took too seriously.

About halfway home, a familiar squeaky voice squealed

from the back of the bus. There was a group of boys playing monkey-in-the-middle with Nathaniel's glasses. "Hey, give me those back. I can't see a thing without them." He circled aimlessly, following anything that moved. Still, the boys, who were bigger than he was, didn't relent.

I hated seeing things like this and I've never been one to hold back. "This isn't right," I muttered under my breath. Moose said something as I left my seat, but I didn't hear it. By the time I got to the back, Nathaniel was reduced to tears. "Alright. Alright. C'mon guys. The joke is over. You did what you set out to do. Give him back his glasses."

The boys stopped and looked me over. The bigger of the kids walked right up to me, "Says who?"

I mulled over which snappy comeback to use. "I do. Well, me and the tooth fairy. She really wants to remind you to brush your teeth." I waved my hand in front of my nose. The kids around us busted out laughing.

This didn't help the big kid's mood. "Well, I don't think you have the guts to make me give the glasses back. Besides, there are three of us and only one of you, *new* boy." He pushed my shoulder back with his hand. "Do you think you can take all of us?"

I knew the odds. I chuckled obnoxiously loud, which again didn't sit well with the biggest kid. "Probably not." I looked over my shoulder towards Moose, who was looking on. "But I think *we* can."

Moose's big paw pressed on the padded seat back, easily squishing it down as he stood up. The entire bus grew silent. He waited there a second peering at us from the darkness under his cap, his lip curled. Finally, he walked towards the back of the bus and stood right behind me.

Two of the boys immediately sat down. The bigger one

explained nervously, "I was...I mean we were just having a little fun. You get it, don't you?"

Nathaniel stood up and snatched the glasses from his hands. He wiped the fingerprints from the lenses with his shirt and put them on. He turned to nod to the boy as if to say *thank you* and without warning, punched the kid square in his nose—sending him sprawling to his seat.

We watched in astonishment, which quickly turned to laughter. "Nice shot, Nathaniel," I said patting him on the back. Moose nodded his head in agreement and returned to his seat. I turned towards Nathaniel again, "Are you okay?"

He dried his tears on his shirt and nodded his head, feeling good that he had the opportunity to stand up for himself. He looked down at his aching hand and whispered, "I've never hit anyone before." He paused, "I think I liked it."

The bus slowly pulled up to the bus stop. Nathaniel and I waited as Moose took his time getting off. Nathaniel looked like he had something on his mind but was having trouble getting it out. Finally, he spoke, "Hey guys. No one has ever stood up for me before. Thanks a lot." Tears started to well again in his eyes. "I know this is stretching it a little, but do you think we could hang out once in a while?"

Moose stared down at him, emotionless. I looked up at Moose and then back at Nathaniel. "I don't think those guys will be messing with you anymore. And, yes," I said.

"Yes, what?" Nathaniel asked getting his composure back.

"Yes, we can hang out sometime."

Nathaniel eyes widened even more through those thick lenses. "Really? That would be great!" He squealed throwing one fist into the air. Then, the same station wagon that dropped Nathaniel off in the morning pulled up. "That's my mom. I better get going. See you guys tomorrow." He extended the arm to his backpack, ran off, and jumped into the car.

I stood for a moment watching. "You're a nice kid," Moose complimented, to my surprise.

"Thanks. You're not too bad yourself, when you aren't scaring the life out of everyone."

Moose cracked a smile. We walked together quietly. It was clear he still had a lot on his mind. I couldn't help to think about if his home life was really that bad. We stopped in front of my house. I couldn't help releasing a little sarcasm, "Well, here we are – the old Henderson home. You know, where strange things happen." I waved my arms in the air and curled my fingers back and forth like I was performing a magic trick.

Moose didn't smile. He stood for what felt like the longest few seconds of my life looking over my home. Etched in his face a seriousness loomed even though I couldn't see his eyes. His jaw locked. "Moose? Hello, Earth to Moose."

Without breaking his glare, he uttered, "Listen. What are you doing in a little bit?"

"Nothing really. I promised my mom I'd start unpacking the boxes in my room. Why?"

Moose swallowed hard, his gaze still fixed, "I need you to come over and," he paused now looking at the top of my house, "help me with a few things, if you don't mind."

"Sure. That beats unpacking boxes any day. Where do you live?"

Suddenly, a deep growl came from behind us. *Spike.* He was angrier than before. His head hung low and the hair on his neck stood up like so many needles. His focus? Moose. He backed up a few steps which only triggered a fit of barking. I had to do something. I tried to whistle at him to distract him. At first, it didn't work. But then, suddenly, as if seeing me for the first time, Spike stopped barking and sat down, separating Moose and me. I reached out my hand and waited to feel his tongue. After, I patted him on the head.

"You sure have a way with animals," Moose spoke in a hushed tone. "You still want to come over?"

"Sure," I said scratching Spike behind his ears. "Where do you live?" Moose loosened his stance a bit and started to walk towards me which only triggered Spike again and sent Moose running. I yelled after him, "Where do you live!?"

Moose's large body surprisingly moved with ease. "Right next door!" He shouted back.

I stood there in awe, watching as Moose unlocked the side door and darted inside. Well, it felt fitting that the mystery that is Moose Oleadertag should live in the only house on the block that was a mystery itself in its appearance. There was so much that I felt needed explaining about both. I looked over his yard and wondered about Moose's story even more.

Spike relaxed once Moose was gone. He really did seem like a nice dog, but something about Moose really bothered him. "He's really not that bad, huh, boy?" With Spike at my heels, he followed me up the wooden porch steps that led to the wrap-around deck. I commanded him to stay outside, and he listened. I rewarded him with some leftover takeout from the kitchen. I wondered if my mother would let me keep him since I made the sacrifice of moving from Akron, right? It was the perfect angle to use to persuade her that I needed a companion.

CHAPTER SEVEN

MR. HENDERSON AND NANUK

I CHANGED OUT OF MY "SCHOOL" clothes and into clothes I could hang out in. I threw my t-shirt on as I walked over to window that overlooked Moose's yard. Words couldn't adequately describe the condition it was in. The trees, the bushes, and the ivy grew out of control and covered the house so much so that the color of the paint was barely recognizable. Only pale sunlight reflected off covered windows. It was an odd sight to see, but perhaps was just a piece of the puzzle that was Norman "Moose" Oleadertag.

I bounded down the stairs. I barely had my other shoe on when I looked over the den. Boxes upon boxes were carefully labeled. Fragile – Mom's Things. Books – Office. Scott's stuff. I *did* promise Mom I'd help her unpack. I'm sure she wouldn't mind if I went next door, especially after our conversation about going out and making friends. I imagined her reaction upon meeting Moose and chuckled to myself.

I walked into the kitchen and scribbled a note on some

loose paper that was left over from Mom's frantic organizing of her camera bag.

Hi Mom,

I met a friend, and I'll be over there. He lives right next door, so I figured it would be okay. I'll explain later. Sorry about the boxes. If you get home before I do, just holler.

Love, Sam

Leaving the note on the table, I bolted for the front door and nearly forgot about Spike as I tripped over him. "Sorry, boy." I thought I should mention something about him, but I didn't have time. Moose was expecting me. "C'mon boy," I called after the dog. He bounded down the stairs like a pup.

Sitting on the steps outside his side door, Moose waited for me. Watching me come from behind the unruly bushes that divided our houses, he demanded, "Leave Spike there."

"Why?" Spike looked at Moose and dropped his head once again while his tail dropped too. A deep growl built inside of him. "Easy, Spike," I commanded. I understood why Moose didn't want him to join us. I walked him to our side gate, opened it up for him, and led him in. I commanded him to stay and he did, all the while looking up at me with sad eyes. I walked toward Moose, "Boy, oh boy, old Spike really doesn't like you."

"Yeah, well, I don't care much for him either. Follow me." Moose was definitely in a very serious mood.

Leading me through the jungle that was his backyard, the foliage swallowed us. Surprisingly, Moose was very agile, moving through with ease while I struggled to find even footing as I was ducking under branches and spider webs. Several large trees, willows and birches, carved a path through the yard with their large trunks and sweeping branches. The roots of the trees jutted up through the ground like so many baseball bats. Moose looked back at me, "It gets a little rough up here. Watch your step."

I looked at the back of his head feeling a little insulted. "Don't worry about me. I'll be just fine." No sooner had the words spilled out of my mouth a large branch swung at my face. WHACK! I let out a cry and as I began to tumble toward the ground, two strong arms grabbed me. It was Moose. But how? He was a good ten steps in front of me. How had he gotten there so quickly?

"You were saying?" Moose's sarcasm was understood loud and clear. "I told you to watch your step." He righted me and turned to lead the way again. I kept quiet, this time really watching out. We walked through a windy path; Moose still moving at a quick pace, with me still trying to keep up.

Moose finally stopped. "We're here."

"Where?"

He lifted his large hand and pointed up the largest tree in the backyard. I looked hard to see what was up there and finally, it came into focus. A treehouse. It was as high as the second story window of my home. It's probably a good time to confess that I have issues with heights. I don't like them and for some reason, they don't like me because every time I am confronted with them, I want to throw up.

"Are you ready to climb?" Moose asked, I looked at him, ready to come up with some kind of excuse, not really wanting to admit my phobia.

"All the way up there? You couldn't install an elevator or something," I laughed nervously. "Okay, let me just tie my shoe." I bent over. My shoelace was just fine, but I needed to build my nerve. I spoke out loud to convince myself that it was going to be okay. When I stood up, I was alone. Moose was nowhere to be found. I looked around the trunk, but he wasn't there. The wind started to blow through the trees, and it felt as if the branches that hung low started to creep down on me. I spun around nervously. "Moose!?" I called out but the only sound I heard was the whistling through the trees and the sounds of the birds mocking my panic. "C'mon Moose. This isn't funny. I'm kinda freaked out over here." Still no answer. The birds sounded closer and some even flew past my head, so I could feel the wake of their wings in my hair. "MOOSE!" I shouted this time not worrying about hiding my panic.

"I'm up here." Moose's voice called finally, silencing the chaos.

I spun my head up so quickly I nearly gave myself whiplash. There looking over the edge of the tree house was Moose's head looking down at me. "How the heck did you get up there so fast?"

"I climbed," he said.

"Yeah, but how?" This I *had* to know. How had such a big kid climbed the tree so quickly and quietly. I didn't hear a single thing.

"Around the back of the tree are wooden planks nailed into the trunk. Climb that like you would climb a ladder. It's easy."

Walking around the back of the tree, I found the planks. They looked old and not very secure. *It's easy, he says.* I put one shaky foot on the first plank and started the climb. I got up fairly easily just by slowly putting one foot on a plank at a time, after checking if it was stable.

When I was nearing the top, Moose called out, "You're doing great. Just a few more feet. Whatever you do, don't look down."

I hate it when people tell me not to do something. The only thing I want to do is do what I'm told *not* to do. And, that's just what I did. After I secured my footing on the next plank, I looked down. My head started to spin as my grip on the planks started to weaken. Suddenly, my left foot slipped. I found myself holding onto one plank with two hands and barely balancing on one foot. My other foot frantically searched to find something, anything that would help me to find balance. "Arrgh. Moose help me!" I yelled, fear dripping on every word.

"I told you not to look down."

"Not a good time for a lecture."

"Give me your hand."

"If I do, I'll fall."

"If you don't, you'll fall. Trust me. When I count to three, give me your hand. One! Two! Three!" I loosened my left hand and popped it securely into Moose's hand. With both of his hands gripped around my hand and arm, he hoisted me into the tree house.

We both laid on our backs trying to catch our breaths. "Why," I asked between gasps, "would someone put a treehouse so high?"

Moose laughed, "It wasn't always this way. As the tree grew, it just got higher. You okay?"

"I'll live."

Moose regrouped himself. He got to his feet and prowled around the floor of the tree house. I dusted myself off and caught my breath and did a quick study of Moose. He began to pace the floor as if he had something weighing on his mind, and he just had to get it out. Two of the plywood walls had large windows cut out. One faced Moose's house and the other faced mine. It was the window facing my house that Moose kept returning to each time taking a good, long look. Finally, he turned to me and said, "Are you ready to learn about the Hendersons?"

I swallowed hard. I got up and looked around. The window where Moose stood had a nearly perfect view of the back of my home, as if by design. Both backyards painted an interesting contrast. "Well, I waited all day to hear this story. So, if you're ready, let me have it." I settled into the corner of the treehouse and waited for Moose to share.

He took a deep breath and began. "Walter Henderson moved into your house several years back. His daughter and her family owned the home and moved Mr. Henderson in after Mrs. Henderson passed away. Mr. Henderson's daughter only lived in the next town, so it was a great way for Mr. Henderson to be on his own without family being too far away.

"So, the day Mr. Henderson moved in, he was greeted by his neighbors. He directed a group of movers to where each piece of furniture was to go and what rooms to put the carefully labeled boxes in. A very large dog was glued by Mr. Henderson's side. He was so big that if he was to stand on his hind legs, he'd be about the height of an average man and easily match his weight. Mr. Henderson introduced himself to his new neighbors and their son. The son could not take his eyes off the large beast that never left the new neighbor's side. He noticed the boy's curiosity. 'This here is Nanuk,' Mr. Henderson explained. 'He's an Akita. Akitas are Japanese hunting dogs. Did you know that two Akitas can take down Japan's largest bear, the Yezo? Yes, they are great hunters, but more importantly, old Nanuk here is a great companion.' He scratched Nanuk behind his ear.

"Suddenly, the boy was so caught up in the story that he quickly reached out his hand to pet Nanuk. The quick movement set Nanuk into protection mode. He growled and barked at the boy sending him sprawling hard onto the ground with a thud. Mr. Henderson gave a tug of the leash as the boy's parents attended to their son. Mr. Henderson apologized and explained the Nanuk was plenty friendly and that you just have to approach him more slowly until he gets to know you. 'He's very protective of me,' Mr. Henderson said.

"Fighting off the tears that started to fill his eyes with the sleeves of his shirt, the boy stood up and screamed, 'I hate that dog. He's stupid.' Then he looked at Mr. Henderson and yelled, 'I hate that you moved in.' He took off running and slammed the door of his house."

I had to interrupt, "It wasn't the dog's fault or Mr. Henderson's." Moose said nothing but continued with his story.

"Over the next several weeks, the boy's family and Mr. Henderson's relationship began to strengthen. Mr. Henderson began to call them his 'extended family.' The boy's father would help Mr. Henderson with some of the bigger chores. His mother would bring over meals or desserts. All was good between the adults, but with the boy – that was a different story. Ever since the incident that first day, the boy would sneakily go to the fence that separated the two yards and torment Nanuk. Sometimes, he'd just stare and say all sorts of mean stuff right to the dog. Other times, he would kick dirt at Nanuk or rattle a stick along the chain links, setting him off.

"Well, one day after sitting at the fence line watching Nanuk, the boy devised a plan that would surely get back at the dog. He ran into the house and grabbed a package of ground beef and mixed all sorts of things into it: a capful of shampoo, some of his dad's talc powder, half a bottle of his parents' antacid, anything else he could get his hands onto. The boy laughed as he mixed the concoction together, picturing Nanuk eating it, getting sick, and throwing up all over the place."

"Who would do such a thing? A monster?" I questioned more rhetorically.

Moose continued, "When the boy came to the fence line, he called for Nanuk. 'Here boy. Let's be friends. I have a peace offering.' Nanuk, cautious at first, moved towards the fence. 'Here ya go, ya big dummy.' The boy chuckled to himself as he dropped the mixture over the fence.

"Nanuk looked at the mixture and sniffed it. Finally, he took the offering into his mouth and swallowed it in two bites. The boy smiled, pleased with himself. Nanuk looked at the boy as if to say thank you, kicked dirt with his back legs, and trotted off.

"Expecting immediate results, the boy was left disappointed. He hoped Nanuk would get sick right then and there.

"At dinner that evening, the boy got more than he expected. There was a knock at the door. It was Mr. Henderson. He looked confused and sad. The boy's mother asked him to come in and what was wrong. He replied, 'It's Nanuk. He's really sick. He's been vomiting non-stop for the last several hours. He needs to go to the vet hospital.'

"The boy was eavesdropping and could barely contain his excitement. The boy's father offered to drive Mr. Henderson and Nanuk to the 24-hour clinic and insisted the boy come with them. It took all three of them to lift Nanuk's massive body into the car. The drive to the hospital was a brutal one. Nanuk lay in the back of the car with his head on Mr. Henderson's lap. He was dry heaving and hacking the whole ride. The boy began to regret his actions and he could swear at one-point that Nanuk lifted his head long enough to look into the boy's eyes. His eyes asked *why?* The boy couldn't meet his gaze and forced himself to look away. By the time the car rolled into the parking lot, Nanuk's suffering had not subsided. Mr. Henderson's lap was a mess of saliva and blood.

"They spent the greater part of the evening at the hospital only to have Nanuk succumb to the boy's evil deed. Nanuk was dead." Moose paused a moment before continuing, "Mr. Henderson? He was inconsolable."

I sat there listening to the tale, angry and frustrated. Could this really be true? I saved my questions and waited for Moose to continue. He paused for a while gazing out of the cutout window before moving on.

"Two days later the veterinarian, Dr. Talbot, called Mr. Henderson and explained that Nanuk may have been poisoned or had simply gotten into something that ate away at the walls of his stomach preventing any digestive acids from working. The boy's mother asked, 'Who would do such a thing and why?' His parents and Mr. Henderson searched for answers. They asked the boy if he knew what happened, or perhaps, if he'd seen anything. The boy stood in denial, insisting he didn't know anything, but at the same time he could not meet Mr. Henderson's inquisitive stare.

"Three days later, the loss of Nanuk took its toll on Mr. Henderson. He was so heartbroken that he suffered a heart attack. He stayed in the hospital for twelve days before finally being released. The boy's parents and Mr. Henderson's daughter helped take care of him until he regained his strength. He never did.

"Several days after Mr. Henderson had come home, he asked for the boy to come over and see him. Of course, he didn't want to."

"Of course not!" I yelled. "He's a complete coward!"

Moose just kept going, "The boy's mother insisted that he go, explaining that maybe Mr. Henderson just needs some good company. So, reluctantly, the boy went. He walked in and called for Mr. Henderson. A weak voice summoned him from upstairs. When he reached the door, he peered into the room. Mr. Henderson waved him in. As he entered, he noticed on the wall were several hand-drawn, black and white framed sketches. Each picture was of dogs and cats. There was one with a dog at the base of a tree presumably barking at a cat that just stared down at him — satisfied with getting away. Another one, had a cat racing along the top of a fence with a dog chasing it along. A third drawing showed a much larger dog cornering a cat in an alley. Each of the six pictures depicted a different scene.

"Mr. Henderson kept a watchful eye on the boy as he looked at them. The boy was truly interested in the artistry of the pictures. However, it was also a good way to prolong having to talk with Mr. Henderson. When he was finished, he turned to look at the ailing man. The boy found it difficult to meet his sickly gaze. Mr. Henderson looked older and nearly lifeless.

"In a hoarse voice, Mr. Henderson asked, 'Do you like my drawings?'

"'You drew those? They're amazing!' He was being honest.

"Mr. Henderson spoke, 'The battle between the feline and canine is as old as time. It is a challenge for both of them, you know. For the canine, the challenge is to try to catch the feline despite its quickness and agility. For the feline, the challenge lies in the escape. One false move and the canine's powerful jaws will win. Often, the canine is left feeling humbled.'

"The boy never thought about this struggle, but somehow, it made sense.

"'You, my boy, have played the role of the canine, haven't you? The Alpha Dog's struggle for power. But, you, my boy, have cheated. You've erased the line between what is right and wrong,' Mr. Henderson coughed weakly covering his mouth with a handkerchief.

"'I don't understand' the boy asked, searching his own mind for meaning.

"'You see. The feline nor the canine resort to blurring those lines. They rely on instinct to see them through. Not trickery to tip the scales in one's favor either way.'

"Mr. Henderson coughed and as he struggled to breathe, the boy was reminded of how badly Nanuk had suffered because of his actions. It was then that he realized what Mr. Henderson was talking about.

"Mr. Henderson continued, 'You've tipped the scales, haven't you? You have spent much of your young life chasing and hurting others because you simply didn't get your way.' The boy tried to explain, but Mr. Henderson waved his hand, cutting him off. 'Like I said, the struggle between canine and feline is one that is played on even ground. A game of wits. No cheating. No advantages. Each playing to its own strengths. Instinct versus instinct. Do you understand?'

"The boy nodded his head, searching for answers, for explanations but found himself speechless. For a moment he thought of defending himself, but there was no argument that would make any sense. Instead, he dropped his head as a tear fell from his eye and he whispered, 'I'm sorry.'

"The old man didn't respond to his apology. He reached over to his night table drawer and pulled out a folded sheet of faded stationary paper. 'This is a letter that you are to read when you get home.' The boy took it from Mr. Henderson's pale, cool hand and put it into his jacket pocket. 'Boy, leave me. But, on your way out, look at the pictures once again. Study them and understand the delicate balance between canine and feline. The feline has to rely on sharpened instincts as you too must be sharp.'

"The boy did as he was told. As he examined each picture, the drawings moved, playing out each scene like a movie. The dog running along the fence line chasing the cat, and the cat narrowly escaping by leaping to the next fence. A dog stalking a curious cat who found itself in the wrong yard, and the cat escaping by using its instinctual ability to climb. The final picture showed how the dog had chased the cat into the corner of an alley. This time the dog would have its way with the cat. He rubbed his eyes, not believing, as each framed sketch became living art. Upon opening his eyes again, Mr. Henderson's cough worsened and now echoed throughout the room and reverberated off the walls. It was as if Nanuk's painful death was being replayed. Then, a howl filled the room sending a chill into the boy's body. He bolted down the stairs and out of the Henderson house.

"He didn't stop until he was safely inside his bedroom. Taking a deep breath, he pulled the letter out of his jacket pocket and settled onto his bed. Slowly, he unfolded it and took to reading the shaky handwriting.

Dear Boy,

You know that I am sick and don't have much time left. When I pass from this world, a great spell will be cast upon you because of your actions. You have been so ill-natured towards Nanuk and me, and it is time for you to make amends. You stole my only friend.

Since you have played the canine, the Alpha dog, the tables will be turned. You see, dear boy, you will be changed into a feline. You will not age. Your senses will sharpen so that your instincts are that of a cat. Train them well, because no one will be left to help you. Your parents will be swept away. You will be forced to face your natural enemy – the canine.

This will not be a life sentence for you to endure. All can be restored. The spell can be broken at any time. To do this, you must retrieve a magical golden vial of milk that will be tucked away in my attic. Once you have retrieved it, you must use it for a kind act. However, there is one catch. It will be protected by the very thing you have taken away from me, the ghost of Nanuk. You must use your new cunning feline ways to outwit him. Anyone may help you, but please understand that their failure will mean that they too will be swept away.

My hope is that you will have learned a lesson from all this.
Good Luck,
Mr. Henderson

"The boy read the note several times before finally crumpling it up and tossing it into the trash. Well, the next day, the boy's mother woke him up and let him know that Mr. Henderson was taken to the hospital. Over the course of the day, the boy could feel drastic, physical changes happening to him. He could hear distant noises from downstairs. Despite the windows being closed, he could smell the odors and fragrances from the flower beds outside He could see even the smallest objects with clarity. He felt every little shift in the air. He couldn't make sense of what was happening until finally it dawned on him. Mr. Henderson's letter. Flipping over the small overfilled wastepaper basket in the corner of the room, he fished through the papers finding Mr. Henderson's stationary. Was it coming true? Was it at all possible? The boy's head echoed with the sounds around him. It must be happening. He was being transformed into a cat. A human cat. If he was feeling this way, then several things had to have happened. Mr. Henderson was dead, and his parents were *swept away*.

"A sick feeling came over his stomach as he pulled his bedroom door open and started for the stairs. Without realizing there were a pair of shoes at the top, he tripped over them and went tumbling down. Instead of breaking his neck, he managed to land on his feet in a crouched position. He stretched his arms forward, feeling the high-strung muscles in his shoulders and chest. For a moment, he admired the way he felt, temporarily forgetting about his parents. Then, the curse jolted into his mind again. 'Mom? Dad?'

"Of course, there was no answer. Frantically, he searched the house, though he knew he wouldn't find them. He looked at Mr. Henderson's letter again. Tears filled his eyes. 'What have I done?!' he shouted out into the emptiness.

"Rain started to fall outside. The boy ran outside, leaped over the bushes that separated the two yards, and dashed to the front door of Mr. Henderson's house. He put his shoulder to the locked door and with his new-found strength was able to knock it open. Standing in the doorway, he glared up the stairs. His only chance was to face Nanuk. As he ascended the stairs, a howling shook the house as if struck by an earthquake. The boy slowly backed out of the house, his feline senses alive and at high alert.

"Ever since that dreadful day, the boy has spent his time alone and scared. Scared that the Mr. Henderson's spell may never be broken," Moose finished telling the tale.

To be honest, I didn't know what to say. I just stared past him and through the window trying to digest the story. Up until the letter, the story seemed believable, but really? A boy was turned into a cat? The idea was well, ridiculous!

Physically, Moose looked exhausted. It was as if telling the story took something out of him. His shoulders hunched, and his head hung low. Why did this appear so personal? I had this feeling that I knew, but like I said, the story couldn't be true. Could it?

I looked for words to break the tension. "So, is that it?"

Moose's head remained low. "That's most of it. Isn't it enough?"

"You do know that there's no way this story can be true. This type of stuff only happens in movies. I mean sure there was probably some dumb kid who may or may not have accidently killed Mr. Henderson's dog, but the rest is, well, fantasy. Also, it doesn't explain the three families in four years thing you told me this morning or the fact that strange things happen in my house."

With an exhale of his breath, Moose reached into his pocket and fished out a folded piece of worn, wrinkled paper and handed it to me. "What's this?" I asked.

"Open it," Moose demanded.

"Is this what I think it is?"

"Samson please, just open it," Moose resolved to begging.

So, I unfolded it and began reading. It *was* the letter! My hands began to shake as I couldn't comprehend if this was real or some kind of hoax. I asked the question I already knew the answer to, "So, this is Mr. Henderson's letter?"

Moose nodded.

Then, an understanding washed over me like cool rain on a hot day. "You're the boy in the story?"

Moose nodded. His body sunk back.

"You poisoned Nanuk?" Instead of nodding, Moose leaned against the wall looking ashamed. I tried to put pieces together in my mind searching for understanding. "C'mon man. There's no way this story is remotely true. What's next?" I

58

searched for words. "Fairies and vampires? Look, I know there are some issues going on with you. I get it. Like you told me. We're cool. You don't have to come up with some sensational story about how you were turned into a – what did Mr. Henderson refer to it as? A feline? Look at yourself. You're a kid. A big and sometimes scary kid, but still a kid."

Moose righted his posture. "Come here." I walked over. "You want proof? You got it." He grabbed the bill of his baseball cap and paused. Pulling the cap from his head, he revealed closed eyes. Suddenly, he opened them wide. What I saw will never leave me. His eyes were an iridescent green that glowed in the late afternoon sun. His pupils were not that of a human. Instead of being round, they ran vertical from the top of the green pigment to the bottom. Just like a...like a cat.

I found myself falling backwards, startled from the revelation. It was as if the birds that had been perched in the trees around us saw the eyes too, because they screamed and flew away all at once forming dark clouds in the sky. My back found the wall behind me. I stared at him. Scared? Maybe a little. But that's not what I was really feeling. Fascination? Yes, that was it. "Well," I swallowed hard. "That explains why you wear that baseball cap all the time. I think I'm starting to believe you now. Tell me more." My eyes fixated on his.

"I never really could gain access to the attic to try and break the spell. Every time a new family moved in, I *insisted* that they help me. They were all unsuccessful."

Insisted?" I asked.

"More like forced."

"What happened to them?"

"You read the letter," Moose pointed to it.

"Swept away?"

Moose nodded, "Just like my parents."

"To where?"

"I don't know. I'm not sure I want to know, but I swear I hear them at night calling for me in my sleep. It haunts me every day."

"You said there were three families in four years. Did you mean they were *all* swept away?"

"Yes," Moose dropped his head and moved over to the window again, his cap still in his hand. "The first family to move in after Mr. Henderson's death was the Johnsons. I convinced Sarah to help me, but it turns out that she was more curious than smart. She went into the attic without me or any information on what to do. The house remained empty for a year after that, and I grew more frustrated and desperate. Then the Singh family moved in. Monica and Manny weren't any more successful than Sarah. Then the house remained unoccupied for a while. That's when Freddy Sullivan's family moved in. I came the closest with his *help*."

"The guys were telling me about Freddy Sullivan. They told me you stuffed him away in a locker."

Moose paused. He looked at me through those iridescent eyes. "I haven't always been proud of my actions, Samson. You wouldn't know. I'm the one who has to live my life this way. I grew desperate."

"So, what happened to Freddy Sullivan?" Moose's eyes gave the answer. I whispered, "Swept away?" The boys' telling of the story earlier that day started to make sense. "What happens now?"

"Well, nearly four years after this nightmare started, you moved in."

"What does that mean?" I already knew the answer. "What happens if my family goes into the attic?" Again, the answer presented itself as the words spilled out.

"There is only one way to end this, Samson."

"Oh no," I insisted. "You aren't going to get *me* swept away. You were the one that was a total creep, not me. This is your mess. You'll need to scoop your own litter."

"This time it will be different, Samson."

"Oh really? How so?" I felt myself getting worked up.

"It's taken me awhile, but I know how to use my instincts. Before, I tried to force myself to act, but now I know that I need to rely on what I naturally do."

"Oh please. You can't even stand up to Spike."

"Listen, I'm not afraid of Spike." I could tell I touched a nerve there. His eyes began to glow. "It's my instinct to run. I can outwit him anytime I want." I rolled my eyes and Moose took a deep breath. "This time it's going to be different."

"How?"

"I'll have you on my side."

"Huh? How am I going to be of any help to you?"

"When I watched you handle Spike this morning, it was something I'd never seen before. You were so calm, and you knew exactly what to do. I knew that *you* were special. With your wit and my feline instincts, we can do this. I just need your help and this curse will be gone from me forever and my parents will return and hopefully, all the other families, too."

I stood there. I didn't know what to say. Everything that happened today was starting to make sense to me; from the howling I heard overnight to the story of Freddy Sullivan. I wanted to help Moose, I really did, but I wasn't sure risking my mother, and even, Scott was worth it.

Moose's cat eyes began to water up and soon tears trickled down his face. "I haven't seen my parents in four years. I've been living on my own. Although I'm *getting* older, it doesn't really show in my face. It's as if the curse has slowed down the process. Everything else about me is aging. My mind. My body. I've grown bigger than your average 10-year-old," he paused, looking down at himself before continuing. "Okay, much bigger, but it's because I'm a 14-year-old kid trapped inside a 10-year-old's body.

"This time will be different. You see, with those other kids, I forced them to go into the attic. I threatened them. I made them seek out the golden vial. I am responsible for so much bad that I must make it right. This time, I want to work together. Samson, I'm afraid that you may be my last hope." He clapped his baseball cap back on his head but couldn't hide the tears streaming from his face.

Seeing Moose cry was something I hadn't expected. In a short time, I'd seen nearly every side of this big, scary kid. I wanted to help him, but I really wasn't sure how I'd do that. This wasn't going to be an easy decision for me. "Look, I'm going to need a few days to think about this. Is that okay?"

Moose nodded. He understood.

We stood in silence for a few moments. "I have a problem," I said.

"What's that?"

"I don't exactly know how I'm going to get down. I'm scared to death of heights."

A wide smile broke across Moose's face, "Oh, I can take care of that." He grabbed me under my arms and tossed me over his back. "Make sure you hold on." I reached around Moose's shoulders and locked my fingers as tightly as I could without choking him. Moose walked over to the edge of the treehouse. Without any hesitation, he started to scale down the enormous tree. Halfway down he stopped, "How ya doing?"

"I'm not going to lie to you, this is probably the weirdest, yet coolest thing I've ever done." And it was. I thought with my fear of heights, I'd be more frantic.

Moose laughed, "You haven't seen anything yet." As the last word left his mouth, he began scaling down again, but this time he moved faster and circled around the tree."

A little fear crept back in, but it was still amazing. "Now, you're just showing off!" I yelled.

We reached the bottom of the tree. Moose looked back at me still secured to his back, "Are you okay?"

"Yeah, why?"

"Because you can let go now," he laughed.

As my feet touched the ground, I noticed that my knees felt a little shaky and my stomach a little queasy. I gathered myself. "I'd better get going. I'll talk to you later?"

"Sure." As I turned to leave, Moose added turning solemn again, "Hey Samson, don't tell anyone about this."

I laughed, "Yeah, like anyone would even believe me."

I waved to Moose and made my way through the jungle and back home. I stood outside looking at my house, now with different eyes. Something was living there, and I knew that it had to go. I knew that I had to help Moose, but this was huge. Did I have what it took to help Moose? And, was helping him worth risking my family? Answers escaped my mind and my thoughts swirled as I walked through the front door.

CHAPTER EIGHT

THE ATTIC

CONVINCING MOM TO keep Spike was easier than I had expected. Back in Akron, I couldn't have a dog because we really didn't have the backyard for it. Also, with the state of our family over the last few years; with my dad being sick and my mom taking it so hard, it really wasn't the right time. My dad and I would talk about how, when he got better, he would get me a dog. "It's going to have to be a small one, you know. And, you're going to have to take it for walks and clean up after it." He would put his hand on my head and mess up my hair. Of course, he never did get better, and the rest is history.

My mom did mention that Scott would have to make the final decision on Spike which gave me about three days to get him trained and into a routine. That was going to be pretty easy considering that he was already an obedient dog.

I woke up, walked into the kitchen, Spike right at my heels, and let him out in the backyard to take care of his business. Noticing Mom didn't make breakfast this morning, I grabbed a box of cereal and a bowl. It was then I realized that I hadn't heard from her at all. A wave of panic washed over me. The curse! Nanuk! I dropped the box of cereal on the table, leaving it to spill on the floor and ran out of the kitchen and up the stairs. The folding attic ladder remained flush against the ceiling. "Mom?" I called. It was silent. This time with a little more panic in my voice I called towards the attic door, "Mom!"

Just then, the door to my mother's room opened and out she came. "Yes, Samson. What's up?"

Feeling relieved, I responded, "Umm, nothing."

"Why are you looking at the attic door? Did you think I was up there?" she chuckled.

I laughed nervously. "Why would I think you were up there?"

My mom laughed back, "Why else would you be staring up at the attic door?"

"I was...umm...wondering how much room there is up there is all. We have so much stuff," I tried to cover up my fear with nervous laughter.

"Yup, we have a lot to store up there and I'm not doing that task by myself. That will be an *us* job, not a *me* job. I was thinking about heading up there this afternoon after we get home. See how much storage we have to work with. Perhaps, we can see how much we need to clean up and start putting boxes up there." She must have read the panic on my face. "What's the matter?"

"Umm...nothing. Let's not work on the attic today. It's probably a good idea to wait until Scott gets here." I laughed again, "I mean you and I have done so much already. By the time he gets here, there's going to be nothing left for him to do."

My mother mulled it over for a moment. I thought she bought it, but then she said, "Oh trust me, honey. Scott will have plenty to do once he gets here. We'll get the easy stuff out of the way and leave the tough things for him." She winked, put her arm around my shoulder and guided me down the stairs and into the kitchen. "How did Spike do last night?"

"He did fine," I wasn't really telling the truth. I mean he *did* do fine, but he was clearly uneasy. Throughout the night, I could hear what I assumed to be Nanuk howling in the attic and not wind blowing through the cracks of the house. Every time, Spike would settle down next to my bed, we would hear that howling. Spike would get up, stare at the ceiling and whine. Also, I spent most of the night thinking about Moose's dilemma. His problem now had become my family's problem. I wasn't ready to tell Mom about the story Moose told me. It wasn't like she'd believe me anyway. But I was curious if she heard anything through the night. "How did you sleep?"

As she finished packing up her camera bag, she turned towards me, "I guess I slept okay. It sure does get windy at night though. I could hear the wind howling through the attic again. When Scott gets here, that's the first thing I'm going to have him look at. Maybe he could seal some of the holes up there."

"Or you could call animal control," I whispered under my breath.

"What was that?"

"Nothing," I said forcing a smile.

"Honey, I have to leave a little earlier today. I am meeting with a family about some portraits. Are you going to be able to get off to school okay?"

"Mom, I'll be just fine," I said, rolling my eyes.

She kissed me on the forehead, "You're getting to be such a mature, young man." I blushed. "And, don't think I didn't notice the cereal all over the floor. Make sure you clean that up before going to school," she threw her eyebrows high on her forehead, which meant she was serious. As she was walking out the door, she reminded me, "We're going to start putting the house together today. I need you home right after school. We're checking out the attic."

What was I going to do? Mom was determined on going up into the attic. What would be up there waiting for us? I let Spike in and sat on the couch. He put his head on my lap and stared up at me. "You wouldn't let anything happen to us, would you, boy?" His head turned from side to side as he licked my hand.

I needed to talk to Moose. He may have an idea on how to handle this. We met at the bus stop. He had his cap back on his head, his black and red flannel covering a different shirt, and what appeared to be the same jeans. I needed to talk to him about the problem we're facing.

"Did you think about it last night?" he asked.

"Yeah, that's all I did. Between that and listening to Nanuk's howling throughout the night. Anyway, we have a problem."

"What's that?"

"My mother. She wants to go and clean out the attic. Today!"

"I don't see how that's a problem," Moose righted himself.

"What are you talking about? How is that *not* a problem?" Just then the bus pulled up. It was then that I realized Nathaniel wasn't there. It was probably better that way. We had a lot to talk about and didn't need his interruptions. After we found our seats, I pressed in a whispered tone, "Help me understand how my mother and I going up to the attic is not a problem." I looked around the bus. People shot stares at us. Perhaps, they weren't used to seeing Moose carry on a conversation.

"It's not a problem because it will give you a chance to scope it out. There's really only one dangerous spot in the entire attic."

"Oh, that's good news," I said in a hushed whisper. "The entire attic isn't cursed, just a part of it." Sarcasm dripped from every word.

"That *is* good news. You see the golden vial is tucked away on the far-left end of the attic when you come up the stairs behind an old trunk. The two times I was up there I saw it. I was so close."

"Let me guess. That's also where Nanuk's ghost is, isn't it?"

"Umm, yup."

"Yup? That's all you have to say?" I waited for an answer. "Look, I don't want my mother swept away," I belted out in a hushed tone.

"Shhh! I understand. Neither do I. Just keep her away from it. You stay away from it too. Just check it out and let me know what you think. Together we can come up with a plan."

I remained silent for a long time. This was all too much for me to handle. Finally, I addressed Moose, "Listen, I don't think I can help you in the way you want me to. My family is just too valuable to me. I know you want this thing gone, but I'm not sure how else to help you. Your friendship means a lot to me. So, I will do this. I will scope it out for you and help with a plan, but after that, you are going to have to get it on your own."

Moose dropped his head. "I understand. Just do that, and whatever you do, keep yourselves away from that side of the attic."

We rode the rest of the way in silence. In fact, we were silent the rest of the day.

CHAPTER NINE

SWEPT AWAY

RAIN BEGAN to fall during the bus ride home. Nathaniel, who arrived late to school, wanted to talk the entire ride. I didn't feel like talking except to be polite – I entertained his questions about which comic books I'd read, who were my favorite superheroes, and if I could have one power what it would be, but for the most part I was silent. Moose sat two seats ahead of us. We hardly spoke at all. Something weighed heavy between us and to tell the truth, I wasn't sure how to get past it. I was supposed to venture into the attic today with my mother. I was afraid we'd suffer the same fate as the other families who lived in the old Henderson home. Would we be the fourth family to be swept away?

The rain started falling heavier as we departed the bus. Nathaniel ran off to his mom's station wagon, and Moose and I walked down the street with neither of us making effort to dodge rain drops. We walked in silence. It looked like he wanted to say something but couldn't get it out. In fact, it seemed like he had wanted to say something to me all day.

"What's on your mind?" I finally asked throwing up my hands.

He didn't answer at first. He just looked straight ahead, but so much was riding on his broad shoulders. Well, of course it was. It was something that I could only imagine. But Moose? He was trapped in it like a nightmare that never ends. "Samson," he finally spoke, "I don't think I can do this without your help."

I didn't say anything. For some reason, I knew that he was right. Then, something caught my eye that stopped me dead in my tracks. Moose didn't realize I stopped until he was two or three steps ahead of me. He looked back. "What's the matter?"

I raised a shaky finger in the air and pointed towards my house. In the driveway was my mother's car. "My mom's home already."

"Okay."

"Okay? What if she got started on the attic without me?" I brushed past Moose into the yard and ran up the porch stairs. I fished the key from my pocket, and on the third try my shaky hands found the key hole. I turned the key and opened the door. "Mom? I'm home! Mom?"

As Moose joined me at the door, both of us listened as only the rain answered. On the kitchen table sat her camera bag and purse. The cabinet doors under the sink, where she stored cleaning supplies, were open. I looked up the stairs and there; at the top of the stairs, was the attic ladder unfolded. "She started without me," I muttered to Moose. I tried calling again from the bottom of the stairs, "Mom?! Are you up there?" Again, we waited, hoping to hear her voice. But again, there was only deafening silence.

Out of nowhere, a scream broke its way into the air, "Someone help me!" It was Mom.

I started to sprint up the stairs, when Moose's strong hand grabbed me from behind. "What are you doing?"

"Hello? Did you hear that? My mother's up there!" I tried to get away from him.

"Samson," he held me in place for a moment, "it's my mess. Let me go first," he said, his voice determined.

I nodded my head in agreement. When we got to the base of the ladder, Moose froze. "He's nearby."

"Who?"

"Nanuk." Moose took a deep breath through his nose. "Your mom was definitely up here. I can smell her."

"How do you know what she smells like?" I whispered.

"I know her smell from your clothes." I followed closely behind Moose as he turned to climb the attic ladder.

When we got to the top, we could hear the whirring sound of the attic fan. My mother must have turned it on because it was so dusty up here, I thought. I switched it off and listened. A faint light bulb cast an eerie dull light over the attic. I panned my head from side to side trying to find her, but she wasn't there. On the floor, lay a broom and a dust pan. Not far from that I could see the trunk that Moose told me about. Fear settled into my body. On the wooden planks, I saw my mother's tennis shoe prints in the dusty floor and some sweep marks made by the broom. Her footprints moved towards the trunk. On the trunk, two hand prints lay in the dust. "She must have tried to move the trunk," I whispered to Moose. On the floor her shoes had made scuff marks. Next to them were her hand prints but they looked like they were dragged across the floor. "Did she fall?" What I saw next chilled me to my very core. Not far from where she had been, paw prints rested in the dust. They weren't just your standard dog prints. These were the biggest I'd ever seen. Big as bear prints, they easily dwarfed Spike's prints, and I'd considered him a large dog.

When I knelt down to compare my hand to the size of the paw print, it was then that I had the realization that my mother had been swept away. Suddenly, drops of water fell by my hands. The rain? A leak in the roof? Through the silence of the attic, I heard my mother's voice. Not in the attic, but somewhere else. "Samson! Samson! RUN!" I looked up and in the pale light of the attic and stared right into the face of Nanuk as drool dripped from his lips. I shuffled my feet to try and get away. Moose grabbed me by my shoulders and dragged me back. Then, he jumped in front of me and threw off his hat. He crouched down and let out a hiss that filled the entire attic. Through the dusty air, Nanuk's teeth showed but Moose wasn't backing off. Suddenly, Nanuk let out a howl that completely shook the house and nearly knocked me to the attic floor.

I grabbed Moose's arm and yelled, "C'mon! Let's go!"

"I got this," he yelled back, trying to free himself from my grip. "I'm going to go for the vial."

"Are you crazy? Let's go!" I pulled harder on his flannel and encouraged him to move down the ladder. Bolting down the ladder as fast as I could, Moose let out one last scream and followed. I folded up the ladder and pushed the attic door up with all my force slamming it flush against the ceiling. Only aware of my heavy breathing for a moment, I felt for the wall behind me, leaned up against it, and slumped down.

Moose sat, his cap clenched into his hands, muttering to himself, "It was right there. It was right there."

I felt the confusion of what just happened slowly morph into a clearer picture. First my dad and now my mother. I was alone. I looked over at Moose who was still muttering to himself. "This is your fault," I said through gritted teeth. He either ignored me or couldn't hear me. "This is YOUR fault!" I yelled at the top of my lungs. "Everything you touch. Everything you do. It...it...all turns out bad!"

Moose turned his head, his eyes, soaked with tears, glowed through his matted, sweaty hair. "What?"

"You heard me. You are a monster," the words came out through clenched teeth.

"You stopped me. I had a chance to make it all right."

"What made you think, of all the times that this was the time you were going to succeed?!" I yelled back throwing my hands into the air. "I wasn't about to risk getting swept away. If I'm gone, then I won't have a chance to save my mother. Didn't you hear her? She told us to run! Even she thought you didn't have a chance."

"She told *you* to run, not me! I had it!"

"You don't know that. Besides, I was – I *am* terrified!"

After a moment of silence, I stood up, walked down the stairs, and opened the front door. Apparently, my glare said it all. He picked himself off the floor, walked down the stairs, and headed for the door. Looking back at me he tried to reason, "Samson. I-,"

"I don't want to hear it." He walked through the door, and I slammed it behind him.

Spike barked from the basement. Mom must have put him there when she got home. I let him out and found my way to the couch where he joined me. He rested his head on my lap. I cried, feeling more helpless than I ever had.

CHAPTER TEN

THE GHOST AVENGERS

THE NEXT MORNING, I woke up on the couch with Spike curled up next to me. I had cried myself to sleep. I thought about who I could call for help, but no one came to mind. Being new in town, I had no one. The police? How do I explain that? *Mr. Officer. Yes, you got that right. A ghost dog lives in my attic because my creep of a neighbor killed him. Now, he haunts my house and swept my mom away. Oh, yeah. I forgot one detail. That creep of a neighbor I told you about? He was turned into a cat.* I chuckled to myself at how crazy it sounded.

The truth was that there really was only one person who could help me, but right now, I had a hard time even being in the same room with him. I moped around the house all day, every once in a while, looking up the stairs at the attic door trying to think of a plan. The truth was that I was going to need Moose's help, and he was going to need mine.

Spike followed me out onto the porch where I sat on the steps. The rain had stopped overnight, and only puffy clouds dotted the sky. A familiar voice broke the silence, "Hey Samson." Nathaniel looked up at me from the sidewalk his arms filled with comic books. "Missed you at school today. Are you sick?"

"What are you doing here, Nathaniel?" I asked harshly, my voice cutting through the air like a knife.

The tone of my voice must have caught him by surprise because he took a step back. It caught me by surprise, too. The last thing I wanted to do was hang out with anyone. It wasn't like Nathaniel was going to be able to help save my mother. I had bigger problems than trying to make friends.

"Well, you said we could hang out sometime. Then I saw you weren't at school today, so I figured I'd come by and see how you were doing." His nasally voice set my teeth on edge. He walked up towards the house. Spike moved to a seated position and extended his paw out to Nathaniel. He cautiously patted Spike on his head. "Wow, I never thought I'd be doing this. He's always been such a nasty animal at the bus stop."

"That's because you aren't a cat," I said under my breath.

"Excuse me?"

"Nothing. Look Nathaniel, today isn't such a great day. I'm kind of going through something right now."

Dejected, Nathaniel said, "I'm sorry." His smile escaped his face leaving a frown. I felt badly, but it was the truth. Nathaniel turned to walk away.

Then, my mother's voice from our conversation earlier echoed loudly in my head, *you're only going to make friends if you go out and just make them yourself.* "Hey, Nathaniel, wait. I'm sorry. I have a few minutes. Do you want to come in and have a piece of cake? It's not homemade, but it will have to do."

Nathaniel's eyes lit up. He was smiling again. "Sure!" He said bounding up the steps behind me causing Spike to think he was ready to play. He crouched and took off down the steps past Nathaniel and darted around in circles in the yard until he was ready to follow us. "I can't believe this is the same dog," he said in wonder.

While sitting down with Nathaniel, he spoke, "You know, when I was talking about how old Spike here and how he used to be such a nasty animal, you said something strange. You said to me that it was because I wasn't a cat. What did you mean by that?"

I didn't realize he even heard me. I grabbed the cake box, "You wouldn't understand."

"Try me," his voice tried to sound grown-up. "I'm pretty mature for a third grader. My teachers say I'm *very* advanced."

I cut off two big chunks of cake and sat back down. "I can see that, but this is all part of my family crisis."

"Umm...what's a cat have to do with your family crisis. What's it sick or something?"

I laughed. He was pretty smart. "It has to do with the Hendersons, a cat, a dog, and my mother."

Confused, Nathaniel cocked his head the same way Spike does. "Huh? It has to do with the Hendersons?" Then, as if struck by something, he realized he was in the house where *strange things* happen. He whispered, "Ohhh, the people that lived here a long time ago?"

"Yes, Nathaniel." I then found myself telling him an abbreviated version of what happened. I left out some parts — especially the part that Moose was a cat and that he killed Nanuk. Moose wouldn't want that part revealed. I did, however, explain that my mother had encountered Nanuk and she was swept away. "So, in order for the curse to disappear, we have to retrieve this magical golden vial of milk."

When I finished, Nathaniel looked at me in astonishment. He could only exclaim a piercing, "WOW!"

"Yeah, wow. So now you understand why I wasn't in the mood for company today."

"Well, that's totally understandable. So, now what?"

I chomped down on the last bite of my cake. "So, now what? I must figure out a plan to outsmart the ghost of Nanuk and get my life back in order. Simple, huh?" I chuckled with nervous sarcasm.

Nathaniel paused for a moment to swallow the last bite. Then he said something that I completely didn't expect. "It *is* simple."

I nearly choked on the last sip of milk, "Yeah right it is. You didn't see the size of this beast. It made Spike look tiny." Spike lifted his head up and whimpered. "Sorry boy, but it's true." Spike put his head back down. I turned my attention to Nathaniel again.

"Well, your solution *is* simple. In *The Ghost Avengers*, Volume 3, there was a similar story. They found out the solution to their problem is that ghosts that have been ghosts for a long time often crave something they loved when they weren't ghosts. Do you understand?"

I didn't fully get it. I sat quietly trying to make sense of it. It was obvious that my face showed my confusion because Nathaniel continued, after a long squeaky sigh and an eye roll, "Luke Lucky from The Ghost Avengers Team faced something similar to this. He had to bring back triplets from another dimension who were taken there by this ghost, King Pig. They called him King Pig because he had made a fortune in the bacon industry. Anyway, before he was killed, he swore he would come back and get revenge. He did just that."

"Well, how did it end? What did King Pig want?"

"Money! You see, he was very rich, but most of his money he got illegally. I mean who gets that rich on bacon, right? The mob boss that killed King Pig outsmarted him of his money. When King Pig confronted him, that's when that mob boss let ole' King Pig have it." Nathaniel made a weird clicking sound, stuck his tongue out of the side of his mouth, and rolled back his eyes mimicking something dead. "Well, King Pig came back and kidnapped the mob boss's kids and swore he would never give them back. To make a long story short, Luke Lucky confronted King Pig. King Pig's ghost got the upper hand and was about to defeat Luke Lucky when he says to King Pig, 'If you do this, you won't get what I brought for you.' Well, King Pig being greedy, loosened his ghostly grip. Luke Lucky says, 'That's right, Piggy. Go ahead. See that box over there. There's over one hundred thousand dollars in it. I'm the only one with the key. You take me away and you get nothing.'"

Nathaniel continued, "Well, as you can probably guess King Pig let Luke Lucky go, and Lucky threw the key over to where the box was sitting. King Pig rushed over there, opened the box, and rolled around in all that dough like a pig in mud."

Nathaniel paused for a second or two which drove me crazy. "What happened next?"

"I thought you'd ask that," Nathaniel snickered. "While King Pig was distracted, Luke Lucky sprang into action. He put on his ectoplasmic glasses and located where the kids were. With his ectoplasmic ray, he opened up a portal, jumped through, and grabbed the triplets. The plan was nearly perfect until King Pig got wise to what was happening. He charged at Luke Lucky and the kids. Luke Lucky stood his ground. In his hand, he held a device with a trigger on it. Just as King Pig was upon them, Luke Lucky said his signature line, 'It's Gotcha

Time!' and just like that, King Pig was frozen in the air. Then his body spun around and spiraled into a device on the floor."

Confused I asked, "What the heck is ectoplasm?"

"Don't you know anything about ghosts?" Nathaniel asked, amusingly annoyed. "Think of it like a snail. You have seen a snail before, right?" I nodded. "Well, you know that trail of yuck that snails leave behind them? Well, it's the same with ghosts. Where every they go, they leave this sort of trail that tells where they've been."

I waited for a minute digesting Nathaniel's story. "Where are we going to get an ectoplasmic ray? That stuff doesn't even exist. Does it?"

Nathaniel paused for a moment. "Of course, it doesn't exist. Believe me, I've tried building one. That's not the point, Samson. The point is that maybe your solution is to find something that your ghost, Nanuk, craved when he wasn't a ghost. I mean, it's a dog. It can't be that difficult. It could be a chew toy, a pair of socks, or some type of food."

My face lit up, "That's it!"

"What's it?"

"Nathaniel, you're a genius!" Spike jumped up and down next to me.

"Well, I've never been called that before — except by my piano teacher. I told you I was smart for my age."

"You are, buddy. You are! If this works, we'll be the best of friends!" I stopped for a second. "Moose. I have to tell Moose." I turned to Nathaniel, "Listen, you can't tell anybody about this, okay? I have to run over to Moose's house. We'll hang out when this is all over. I promise."

"Who would believe me?" Nathaniel threw up his hands as his thick-rimmed glasses bounced on his nose.

Bounding towards the front door, Nathaniel and I raced to

the porch. As we walked down the stairs, I could see he felt proud of himself. As he turned to walk away, I asked, "Hey, Nathaniel, one more thing."

"Sure, anything!"

"Can you bring *The Ghost Avengers* comic to school tomorrow?"

He stuck a thumb in the air, "You bet!"

I watched Nathaniel skip away. He certainly had a pep in his step. I gazed over at Moose's jungle of a yard. Could this be the solution to everyone's problems? I didn't know, but I was excited at the possibility. As the sun started to set, I led Spike to the backyard, and I darted over to Moose's house calling for him, "Moose! Moose? Get out here. I've got great news. I think we can break the spell!"

CHAPTER ELEVEN

A SLEEP OVER

I STOOD in the middle of Moose's yard for minutes calling for him. Finally, a distant voice echoed through the yard. "I'm here."

"Where?"

"Back here. In the treehouse."

I darted through the yard this time ducking and dodging over roots and under branches until I finally reached the base of the tree. "I think I know a way to get to the golden vial!" Without thinking, I started climbing the ladder and reached the top. I was too excited to think about my fear of heights. When I righted myself inside the tree house, Moose was sitting in the corner under the window that faced my house, his cap by his side, looking dejected. I tried to change the mood, "Moose, I have great news!"

Moose looked up with tears in his eyes, "Samson, I'm so sorry about your mother. I never wanted that to happen, especially to you."

"Didn't you hear me? I think I found a way to defeat Nanuk."

"Samson, I've tried everything. Nothing worked. Nanuk is too agile and too big for either of us."

I softened my voice, "You're right. He *is* too big and agile for either of us. But, he's not as smart as the both of us."

"How is that?"

"This afternoon Nathaniel came over—"

Moose interrupted, "Oh, I bet you're going to tell me that Nathaniel Fargo, the thick-lensed wonder solved the mystery I've been trying to solve for the last four years."

"EXACTLY!" I tried my best impersonation of Nathaniel adjusting my pretend glasses and mimicking a nasally voice, "I'm pretty mature for a third grader."

Moose chuckled, "Well, what's this great idea?"

I proceeded to tell him the entire story of Luke Lucky and King Pig. I explained how ghosts often long for something from their past lives.

"Your plan sounds great, but where are we going to get an ectoplasmic ray?"

"We aren't. They don't exist," I laughed, thinking how I must have sounded to Nathaniel earlier. "The key is finding something that Nanuk craves."

Moose was quiet for a second. "That just might work. We need to come up with a plan though."

"I know we do. We can work on it all night if we have to." I stood at the window overlooking my house as the wind began to howl. "Nathaniel is going to bring the comic tomorrow. We can talk about it at school and then put it into action."

Moose nodded his head slowly, thinking it over. "This may be our last chance. Do you think it will work?

I shrugged. "What other choice do we have? I know one

thing for sure. I'm not sleeping in my house another night by myself."

"I don't blame you. Wanna sleep up here tonight? We've got plenty of sleeping bags and a lantern. Some snacks, too."

Later that evening, we settled into our sleeping bags. Piles of notebook paper, some crumpled into balls and others tacked onto the side of the tree house, rested in the corner. Moose dimmed the lantern. We laid in silence for several moments listening to the wind through the trees and distant howling of Nanuk in the attic.

"Moose?"

"Yeah."

"Why'd you do it?"

"Do what?"

"You know, poison Nanuk?"

Silence settled into the air as if the wind too wanted to hear the story. "I've asked myself that question so many times over the past four years. I really don't know why I did it. I knew it was wrong all along. Maybe it was because I've had trouble getting along with people. I'd have outbursts when I didn't get my way. After my kindergarten year, my parents decided to take me out. I was homeschooled. But, animals? They always liked me. So, when I reached out to Nanuk that day, and he reacted the way he did, I felt completely betrayed. Being homeschooled, I didn't have many friends, and now the only thing I could make friends with was now turning on me. I felt confused about all of this. So, I did what I did."

I took a moment, thinking about what Moose was saying. He really did have some problems. Problems that no one could possibly understand. "So, what was it like to live all these years on your own? Didn't anyone check on you?"

"We really don't have any close relatives. There are a few

that live back east, but we aren't really in touch with them. Being a homeschooled kid, there aren't a whole lot of checkups. So, I flew under the radar."

"How did you survive all this time on your own? I'd be scared."

"Well, my parents have quite a bit of money in the bank. I'm not sure how they got it, but I remember them mentioning something about a settlement. Because I didn't go to school like normal kids, my parents were always trying to teach me about how life works and stuff. They showed me how they use the internet to pay bills and things like that, so I figured they would want me to do all that stuff while they were, ya know, swept away."

"How'd you get all their passwords?"

"Everything is saved on their computers."

"Smart," I thought. I didn't think I'd ever be able to pull that off. Moose was certainly smarter than people give him credit for. "So, how'd you get yourself back into school?"

"Well," he chuckled, "I do know that you can't just show up and pick a class. I learned that the hard way and nearly blew it for myself. If I'd been caught, they would have checked up here for sure. I figured that if I really wanted to break the spell, I would need some help. The only way to do that was to get myself enrolled into school. So, I had to enroll myself."

"How'd you do that without your parents?"

"Again. The internet. Everything is done online. I just answered some questions, turned in the correct paperwork like birth certificate and the electric bill, and made some excuses about why my parents couldn't come in and stuff. It was easier than I thought it would be. After a while, they stopped asking questions. This is my third year now in school. I didn't do enough work the first year, so I had to repeat a year. That worked out great because our paths crossed." He paused a minute. "I'm not stupid, you know. I know the stuff they're teaching me. I'm just so concerned with how I'm going to break this spell that school seems so...so silly and meaningless. But, everyone around me, the other kids and teachers, treat me like – well – an outcast."

I thought about what I wanted to say before I said it. "Moose, you know you make it hard for people to know you. You put on this tough guy act that, and I'm being honest here, scares the life out of people."

"It's easier that way. No one would understand me, and nobody *tries* to understand me."

"Well, for another thing, I don't think you're stupid. You are probably one of the smartest and bravest people I've ever met." We sat in silence for a while. There was another thing that I was curious about, "Moose, how did you get food and learn how to cook and all that?

He chuckled, "I think it was all part of the spell. Since I never really aged, everything else stayed the same. There was always food, you know, like the basic necessities; milk, bread, and sandwich meat. Stuff like that. Each time I would eat it, it would magically be replaced. Even though my parents have money in the bank, I didn't have any *money-money*. I mean they had some around the house, but that didn't last long. So, anything extra I wanted I'd have to steal it. I made sure not to make a habit of it."

"Steal it? Like a life of crime or something? You're like America's Most Wanted." We both started laughing.

"My parents loved the outdoors, so I learned little cooking tricks along the way. I never made anything gourmet, but it was enough to keep me going all these years."

Again, silence found its way into the treehouse. I tried to

make sense of everything and wondered if I would have what it takes to be on my own for so long. "You know what Moose? I like the person you are right now. You're just being you. I consider you my friend. My friend no matter what happens."

No words needed to be said. The wind outside started to blow through the treehouse again. From the attic next door, Nanuk's ghost continued his howling song into the night as if he sensed we were planning on retrieving the vial.

CHAPTER TWELVE

THREE UNLIKELY FRIENDS AND A PLAN

At the bus stop the next morning, the three of us gathered together to look over Nathaniel's comic book. As we talked about some ideas, I looked up at Moose and Nathaniel. I couldn't help to think that just three days ago we were complete strangers. Jan and Pam must have thought the same thing because they stood together, mouths agape, and pointed fingers. I really didn't care what they had to say.

The bus ride, which was oddly quiet, offered more time for us to work on the plan. As I looked around, all the kids must have thought it odd that three completely different people seemed to be three unlikely friends.

At lunch, Moose and I would finalize our plan without Nathaniel since his lunch time was different than ours. He was really the mastermind behind everything, and we would talk with him after school to see if he thought our plans would work. Moose certainly realized that Nathaniel was much smarter than your average third grader. Heck, he was smarter than your average middle-schooler. I had seen a different side of Moose too. He was smarter than he let on and a lot kinder than his rugged exterior.

I sketched up a map of the attic complete with where the trunk sat. I colored a gold color where the vial of milk was in bright rays like sunshine. We talked over different scenarios and tried to come up with solutions to each one. "So, Moose, since you know Nanuk so well, what is it you think will be the one thing he craves?"

"I've been thinking about this all day. The only thing I can think of is the one thing that I killed him with."

"Meat?"

"Yes, I used to watch Mr. Henderson give him ground beef rolled up into little balls. That's where I got the idea to try to make him sick."

"Then meat it is!"

"You think it will work?" I questioned.

"It has to," Moose nodded and shrugged his shoulders.

After the last bell sounded, all the student body gathered in the hallway, racing to head home. In the middle of the throng, Moose and I walked side by side. Butterflies danced in my stomach. Nervous? Yes, yes indeed. If we failed, I may never walk these hallways again. We may never see our families again. If we failed? I let that question go for now. I could not let doubt get to me.

As for Moose? Something was different about him today. He didn't lumber through the hallway like he usually did. He had a pep in his step. I even had a hard time keeping up with him. He was his usual silent self, but there was something different. Confidence? Perhaps. Maybe for once, he didn't feel as if he was on this journey alone. Maybe he felt as if he finally was able to master his feline instincts, and he felt sharp. Maybe this time, he felt that they had a chance to break the spell. Whatever it was, it was clear that Moose was different.

On the bus, Moose and I filled Nathaniel in on what we talked about at lunch. He listened approvingly. We sat whispering about the final details. I would prepare the meat when I got home. Once that was set, so were we. Finally, the bus pulled up to the stop. The trip home felt much faster than usual, as if the bus knew that we had a showdown planned with Nanuk.

Nathaniel's mother waited in her gray station wagon. He looked up at us, "Good luck, fellas. I wish I could be there with you."

We both nodded. We wished he could be there too, but we also knew it was no place for him to be. Earlier that day, we had come up with a friendship handshake that involved a few various movements and finished with a high-five. We did it with Nathaniel. He smiled through his thick glasses and was off.

Moose called out, "Hey Nathaniel?"

"Yeah?"

"It's Gotcha Time!" Nathaniel beamed and threw a fist into the air before he got into his car. It felt good to laugh. It helped to push aside the anxious feeling that made my stomach flutter. I think Moose felt the same way.

We walked together. With each step closer to the house, that nervous feeling grew again. I felt my hands getting sweaty. Moose? He looked as calm as ever which helped me a little. Standing in front of the house, the skies began to open up and rain started to fall. We ran to the porch. I ran around to the side gate to get Spike. Grabbing his collar, I rushed him inside. As he passed Moose, he growled. Moose didn't run this time. No, this time he crouched, ready for what Spike may do.

I directed Spike into the kitchen, and he listened. After Moose helped me move some unpacked boxes in front of the kitchen doorway so Spike couldn't get out, he waited in the living room, so I could prepare the bait. I moved quickly to the refrigerator and pulled out the meat. Mom planned on making my favorite this week: sloppy joes. I rolled up several balls of the cold, raw meat. Spike, at my side, begged for a sampling. I didn't disappoint him. I tossed him a piece and he gobbled it up licking my fingers to make sure nothing was left on them. I hoped Nanuk would want the meat as much as Spike did.

I met Moose in the living room as he pushed the boxes back into place. Spike growled and barked at the mere presence of Moose even though he couldn't see him. We stood at the bottom of the steps looking up at the attic door. Without hesitation, the plan was a go. Moose reached up and grabbed the latch and unfolded the attic ladder.

CHAPTER THIRTEEN

NANUK, MOOSE, AND THE GOLDEN VIAL

THE DIM, hanging light bulb was left on from the last time we encountered Nanuk. Moose led the way with me closely behind him. Our heads peeked into the attic, panning left and right. It appeared as if all was safe. This seemed too easy. Was the only thing we had to do was race on over, grab the golden vial, and get out of the attic?

Rain pelted away at the roof above which intensified the eerie atmosphere. The dust had settled from the day before. On the floor, the faint footprints of my mother and Nanuk still lay visible.

To the left, the black trunk rested. A few feet from the trunk, water leaked from the roof. "Remind me to tell my mother that the roof needs to be fixed." Moose ignored me. His nose twitched smelling the air. His senses were on high alert. "Is he here?"

Moose paused. "I don't sense him." We moved into the attic and towards the trunk. Behind it, we could see a glow. "There it is."

"Okay, so now what?"

"I'll move the trunk. You reach behind it and grab the vial."

I nodded. It was as good a plan as any given that Nanuk wasn't there. Moose bent over and pushed the trunk. At first, it didn't budge. Moose shouldered it again, and it finally moved. I looked behind it. There it was. The golden vial of milk! It glowed so brightly that it caused me to squint. I reached my arm behind the trunk as far as I could, but it was still just out of my reach. "I need a little more space, Moose." He shouldered it again.

Out of nowhere, I felt warm air on my face. I froze. A bark echoed through the attic. My hair was pushed back with each one. Nanuk's mouth started to take shape and I could see lips curled back to reveal his teeth. Before I could react, his mouth opened and engulfed the top half of my body. I struggled with my feet to keep from being swept away. Inside his enormous mouth, I tried to focus. The darkness gave way to a foggy light. The moisture of his mouth soaked my body and filled my nose, ears, and mouth. I could see images of the ghostly legs of people and felt their hands grasping my shoulders and pushing me out of Nanuk's mouth. Even though I was being pushed, it was as if there was no hope as my legs had lost their footing. It was inevitable, I was going to join the others in being swept away.

Suddenly, I felt two strong hands yank my ankles, and with help from those inside Nanuk, I was released from his jaws. I landed in a sloppy heap. This must have been the ectoplasm that Nathaniel referred to. I heard Moose hiss loudly like a big cat. His large hands dragged me behind him. Dust kicked up all around us. Moose crouched and continued to hiss and growl. Removing his cap, he revealed his glowing eyes, which shone bright through the dust in the direction of

Nanuk's barking. By the sounds of it, they were both ready for a fight.

As the rain pelted down on the roof, I could hear Spike barking from downstairs. Nanuk's ghost started to materialize. Moose, bent at the knees, was about to head into the direction of Nanuk. I felt fear settle into me. I started to doubt whether we would be successful. I tried to pull Moose back. He grabbed my hand and looked at me, his eyes causing me to squint, "Samson, let go of me," his growl so deep, I knew he meant business. "I've got this!" I let go of his arm.

Nanuk released a howl, that echoed into our ears, and he lunged at Moose. Moose dodged and took a swipe at him, making contact with his nose. The giant dog lunged, and Moose scaled the wall and landed on his feet. Nanuk's body crashed into the trunk. Between the hissing and the barking, the noise was deafening. Nanuk lunged again. Moose hissed and darted out of the way making sure I was behind him. Moose was countering Nanuk's movements, but Nanuk's persistence began to tire Moose. Realizing this, Moose and I darted towards the stairs. We couldn't retreat now, could we? I suddenly remembered *The Ghost Avengers* plan. "Moose, it's time for the plan!"

Moose scanned the attic. It was suddenly quiet. "Where's the bait?" he whispered.

"Right here," I pulled the sandwich bag from my pocket and took out the meat.

The rain intensified outside. Wind filled the cracks of the attic, and the sound pierced through me. Spike continued barking. "Okay, on the count of three, throw it towards the opposite corner."

I pulled out one ball of meat, held it in my hand, and readied it. Side by side, we walked toward the trunk again. We stopped, waiting for the right time. In the hollowness of the attic, we heard Nanuk's ghost begin his low growl. His enormous paw prints formed in the dust on the floor. Each one moved slowly, closer to us. This was it: the final showdown. Drops of Nanuk's saliva fell next to the enormous paw prints. His growling turned into raging barking. Before our eyes, Nanuk's ghost appeared again. His curled lips revealed his saliva-drenched teeth.

Moose's eyes glowed with anticipation as he crouched. This time, there would be no backing down, no running away. I held the meat out in my hand. Nanuk's barking and growling stopped and only the rain, wind, and Spike's distant barks sounded through the attic. Nanuk sniffed the air and his face softened. His attention turned to my hand. I threw a small piece of meat to the floor in front of him. He bowed his head, first sniffing the meat and then devouring it. He focused his attention to us again.

"It's working," I whispered.

"Ready?" Moose placed his hand on my shoulder.

We looked at each other and nodded. "It's Gotcha Time," we said in perfect unison.

"On three. Ready? One...two...THREE!"

I held the ball of meat over my head and whistled the way I had with Spike that first day at the bus stop. Nanuk followed my hand. I threw it to the far corner of the attic. Without hesitation, Nanuk's ghost turned and ran towards the meat, just as we hoped.

Moose and I sprinted over to the trunk. "There it is, Moose!"

"No time to look at it, grab it!" Moose thundered.

I scurried behind the trunk, secured the vial, and handed it over to Moose. We started to run towards the stairs. Before we took our third step, Nanuk's howling shook the entire house. His rage intensified as if he knew he'd been tricked. He was a few paces away from the stairs and was approaching us slowly, his head down and growl intensifying with each step.

"We have the golden vial!" I yelled. "Why isn't the spell broken?"

"I don't know. I've never gotten this far before." Moose crouched, his eyes glowing brighter. A deep growl echoed like that of a lion. This was indeed the final showdown. Winner take all. Understanding what was about to happen, Moose yelled at Nanuk, "I did what you asked of me, Mr. Henderson! What more do you want?!"

Nanuk now blocked the attic ladder down towards the safety of the house. Moose handed the golden vial back to me. He looked at me wistfully for a moment as if to say *thank you for everything*. He turned to face Nanuk, this time on all fours. Nanuk's barks grew louder. His teeth appeared sharper. The two moved closer to each other, nearly nose to nose. As Nanuk crouched and leapt towards Moose, a flash of black barreled into Nanuk's body, sending him crashing into the wall. Spike! Nanuk righted himself, towering over him. The two faced off, each growling and baring their teeth. Their bodies collided into each other as they rolled towards the far corner of the attic.

This was our chance. Moose grabbed me by my shoulder and shoved me past the fighting dogs and down the stairs. Out of the corner of my eye, I caught a glimpse of Nanuk standing over Spike's body. Spike let out a piercing cry. When our bodies hit the floor below, I looked up as Spike was thrown across the attic above. Moose reached up and started to fold the ladder. Before it closed completely, Spike's body came tumbling out of the entry and slammed onto the carpet – battered, bloodied, and motionless.

We both sat on the carpet looking over Spike as we struggled to catch our breath and tried to make sense of what had just happened. Beside me sat the golden vial of milk, shining brightly. "Did we do it?" I asked breathing heavily. "Do you feel different?"

Moose surveyed himself. "I don't feel any different. My feline senses are still on high alert. I can still feel the presence of Nanuk's ghost."

"Where did we go wrong?"

"I don't know." Moose sounded defeated.

Just then, Spike let out a whimper. I looked him over. Concern crept into me. "He doesn't look good, does he?" I knelt down next to him and with my sleeve already wet from being inside Nanuk's body, I wiped the blood from Spike's mouth. Tears flowed from my eyes as I embraced him, not knowing if he would survive. With my head on his chest, I could hear his struggle in every breath.

Moose joined me. Reaching over, he grabbed the golden vial of milk and placed it next to Spike's head. He lifted his head off the floor. Moose poured some into Spike's bloodied mouth. I scratched Spike's fur encouraging him to drink. I looked up at Moose, "I hope he's going to be..."

I couldn't believe my eyes. Sitting up against the wall was Moose. Not the ten-year-old Moose I'd met just a few days ago, but a much older fourteen-year-old Moose. The red and black flannel he was wearing now fit tightly and the cuffs rode up to his elbows. His jeans now looked like a long pair of shorts. His toes ripped through his canvas, already tattered, shoes.

He sat there and looked down at his body in amazement. In a deep, raspy voice, he uttered, "It's working." His eyes widened not recognizing his own voice which had taken on a deeper tone. He tried it out again, "The spell. It's breaking. We did it!" We both jumped to our feet. *R-I-I-I-P*. Moose's flannel tore right down the back.

As we stood side by side, Moose was even taller now. "Wow, Moose. You're...you're...old!"

"Oh yeah?" he countered. "It's better than that ooze dripping all over you."

I looked down at the pinkish ooze on my arms and shirt. My hands ran through the slop in my hair. "I think some got into my mouth." I stuck out my tongue. "Bleh." We both started laughing.

Regardless of the mess that was all over me, Moose picked me up and spun me around in circles — careful not to step on Spike. "We did it. I knew today was the day!"

Just then, there was a scratching coming from the attic. We looked at each other in shock. If the spell was broken, then why was Nanuk fighting to get out of the attic?

CHAPTER FOURTEEN

REUNION

THE SCRATCHING TURNED INTO BANGING. We looked at each other in bewilderment. Nanuk? Suddenly, a voice called out, "Samson? Are you there?"

"Now, Nanuk can talk?" Moose asked in disbelief.

"No, man. That's my mother!"

Moose reached up and pulled down the ladder. At the opening inside the attic, my mother stood there with tears in her eyes! "Mom!" I bolted up the ladder and into her arms.

She hugged me tightly. "I saw what you did. You were so brave."

"You saw?"

"Yes. Who do you think was trying to push you out of Nanuk's mouth? You and your friend were very brave." She gave me another hug. "We still have one problem."

"Uh-oh. What's that?" I looked at Moose who had joined us back in the attic.

"We still have a lot of cleaning up to do," Mom stated as she pointed to the side of the attic where the trunk lay.

My mouth dropped open in astonishment. The attic was full of people. I looked up at Moose. He was smiling from ear to ear. "I guess I should introduce you to everyone. First of all, hello, Mrs. O'Keefe. I'm Norman. My friends call me Moose." With that, he put his arm around my shoulders and shuffled through the crowd. "These people here are the Johnsons and this is their brave daughter, Sarah. Next, we have Mrs. Singh, Monica and Mandy. And finally, we have the Sullivan family, and this guy right here is Freddy." Exhaling deeply, Moose addressed everyone in the attic making sure his now human eyes met theirs, "I can't express how sorry I am for what I've done. I'm ashamed that my actions affected each and every one of you." Then, as if he could see something in the distance of the attic, he added, "And to you, Mr. Henderson." He smiled as tears welled in his eyes, "And, of course, to you too, Nanuk."

"What about us?"

Norman froze in his tracks, recognizing the voice although he hadn't heard it in a long time. He turned. "Mom! Dad!" He raced right into their arms. Tears flowed freely from all three of them.

"Norman, we are so proud of you!" Mr. Oleadertag cried.

Just then a dog barked from behind them. Everyone stiffened but me. I knew who it was. It was Spike, and he was healed. I knelt down, and he darted towards me licking my face and letting me scratch behind his ears. "May I?" Moose stood behind us. He extended his hand out to Spike. Ignoring his hand, Spike jumped into his arms and showered him with kisses. I guess he and Moose were also cool.

I looked back at Mom. She walked over to Spike who was now by my side. "I saw what he did too. So brave," she said patting the top of his head. "I'm more than happy to say that he's definitely part of our family." Mom smiled from ear to ear while holding me close. I was never going to let go.

EPILOGUE

It's been a few years, since the events in the old Henderson house. Scott and Mom married and as a stepdad, I have to say he's alright. My mother is happy. The job he moved out for turned out to be a good deal for us. He was quickly promoted and runs the company. My mother is doing great as a photographer. She's even won some contests and stuff like that. It's hard to take a bad picture on the shores of San Diego. She's well sought after and has been booked for endless events. We tried several times to explain what happened that day in the attic, but Scott laughs it off. He doesn't doubt that something went on, but he doesn't believe it all. Truth be told, it *is* a tough story to swallow. So, Mom and I keep it as our secret.

All the families that used to live in the old Henderson house relocated. After the events of the attic, they were different people too. Turns out they didn't want the house back. Who would blame them? While they were swept away, Moose used the internet to arrange for movers to store all their stuff before the next family moved in. They were grateful and surprisingly forgiving for the events in the attic.

Nathaniel went on to do some great things. With lots of confidence after facing off against those bullies on the bus, he convinced his overprotective parents to sign him up for karate. He's now a blackbelt, if you could believe that. He and I have remained friends and spend lots of time combing through comic books. He's even started writing and illustrating one based on what happened in the attic. It's pretty good, but I'd be lying if I wasn't partial to the storyline. He never did get rid of those glasses, he says that they're his trademark.

Norman? He never did go back to being called by his real name. Obviously, he and his parents had a lot of catching up to do. With Scott and Mom's help, they cleaned up their yard and the inside of the house. It turns out that one of the advantages of living alone all those years is that no one is badgering you to clean up after yourself. Our families had grown close and our parents spend a lot of time together barbequing or going out. I guess such a crazy experience has a way of bringing people together. Moose and I remain close. We've spent countless hours up in the treehouse. It's safe to say that I don't have any problems climbing that rickety old ladder anymore. Sometimes, we look out of that window and stare at the attic of my house. The stories never get old and we talk about the "what ifs" of that day. We laugh out loud, but there are times when we just sit in silence. That day changed us. Deep down, we are thankful for Mr. Henderson and Nanuk.

Over the last year or so, we haven't hung out as often as we used to. Moose is nearly done with high school. He had a lot of catching up to do which he managed with tutors and summer school. That night gave him a new lease on life, and he wasn't wasting it. It turns out that even though he was transformed back into a human, he didn't lose *all* his quickness and strength. He has several scholarship offers from colleges for wrestling. Who wouldn't want a state champion?

Moose and Nathaniel weren't the only ones changed by what happened in the attic. After Nanuk tried to devour me, it turns out that some of his ectoplasmic ooze did get into my mouth as well as every other hole on my face. I've not felt myself since those events in the attic. Most nights, especially when the moon is full, Spike and I like to sit on the porch, let my new senses take in the world around us, and sniff the night air. I never get the urge to chase a car like old Spike does, but something inside me sure enjoys a game of catch.

Everyone was right. Strange things certainly happened in this house. But without these strange things, my first days here wouldn't have been so much of an adventure and this house wouldn't have felt like a home so quickly.

ACKNOWLEDGMENTS

I want to thank all the people who had to hear about the attic for the past twenty years; my family, friends, and students. To Lisa, Megan, Andrea, and Avery, thank you for editing this complete mess of a book and making it something at the very least – readable. Next, to Erica, my first reader from my intended audience. Thank you for your feedback. It was really helpful! Finally, to Veronica, my wife and bestie, thank you for your patience and listening to this story and others, and allowing me to bounce ideas off of you. Thank you for encouraging me to keep at it.

ABOUT THE AUTHOR

Born in New York and raised on Long Island, Solomon Petchers has an affinity for scary stories where friends come together to defeat whatever bad guy or entity they face. It's no wonder that Stephen King is his favorite author. After getting his teaching degree, he moved to Southern California, where he's spent all of his 23-year career in education. Currently, Solomon lives in Murrieta, California with his wife, Veronica, and three amazing children. When he's not writing or teaching, Solomon spends time with family and going on dates with his wife. Their choice of movie? Anything suspenseful or outright scary!

You can visit him at: www.solomonpetchers.com

56474599R00068

Made in the USA
Middletown, DE
22 July 2019